OUT OF BODY

OUT OF BODY

THE
BELLWEATHER TRILOGY
BOOK ONE

QUINN ELLIS

GEMINI
PRESS

GEMINI
PRESS

Out of Body, Quinn Ellis

ISBN: 978-1-9558-5810-6
Library of Congress Control Number: 2023930422

librapress.com

XVIII

THE MOON

ONE

Kimmie clung to the banister, nearly slipping as she struggled to pull herself forward through the icy water that kept trying to suck her under.

It took everything she had to plant her numb foot on the next step. She glanced back at the dark whirlpool where there had once been stairs and whimpered. She'd be sucked down the staircase, into the flooded ground floor if she let go. And there she would drown.

This isn't real. This isn't real. This isn't real.

But no matter how many times she told herself that, the water kept rising. Even if she made it to the attic, she still might die. The second floor would be underwater soon, and if she couldn't find a way to break through the roof …

A wall of water slammed into her from behind, tearing her free of the banister and slamming her hard against the wall, knocking the air from her lungs before yanking her down.

Don't breathe.

She flailed against the water that tumbled her over and over in the darkness. Her hand hit something, but the water snatched it away before she could grab it before.

Phosphorescent dots swam in her vision. Her lungs burned for air.

Don't breathe.

The water was slower here, but Kimmie's arms didn't want to move. And which way should she go anyway? She'd never make it back up, and there was no way out down here.

Don't breathe.

But she couldn't help it. Her lungs spasmed. Frigid water filled her mouth and nose, burning and numbing in unison. The current shoved her down and pinned her to the floor. The glowing dots faded, and for a moment, Kimmie faded too.

Then the water washed her up on a shore of stained hardwood floor.

See? You're dreaming. All you have to do is wake up.

She coughed out water, then sat up. There were cobwebs in every corner of this dilapidated parlor, but the old-fashioned furniture didn't look nearly as dusty as it should. The room felt familiar, even though she was sure she'd never been there.

But someone else had, and not long ago.

The overstuffed loveseat held wads of plastic sheeting; the kind painters used to protect things from splatters. The fancy carved coffee table was littered with empty beer bottles and junk food wrappers. Several pizza boxes had been stacked on an end table.

From Antonio's, which had gone out of business when Kimmie was still in middle school.

She opened the top box, expecting to see moldy crusts. Or cockroaches. Instead, she found one slice of pepperoni pizza. It looked edible, if greasy.

The whole scene felt less like squatters and more like an interrupted party.

Footsteps on the staircase that had been a raging whirlpool a minute ago.

Maisie.

The girl who'd been killed at the Bain house eight years ago. Kimmie remembered the pictures on the news — she'd been stabbed on prom night, and the killer had never been caught.

Shit. This was one of those dreams.

"Please," Kimmie heard herself beg as she backed toward the door at the back of the room. "Please let her go."

What did that mean?

This is your dream. You're in control. Teleport to the beach.

But nothing changed no matter how hard she tried to visualize herself on a beautiful tropical beach with crystal clear water. Lucid dreaming techniques didn't work in those dreams.

Wake up. Wake up. Wake up!

"You shouldn't have warned them," Maisie said.

But not like Maisie would've said it. Kimmie didn't know how she knew that. She'd never met Maisie when the girl was alive.

"I needed seven," Maisie added.

Kimmie lunged for the door, throwing it open and bolting inside the tiny room behind it. She looked around frantically for something she could use as a weapon, but everything was covered in plastic: two small chairs on either side of a desk. Shelves full of mildewed books. A chipped crystal ball with a jagged crack running through it.

Maisie appeared in the doorway. "She doesn't want me to hurt you."

3

Kimmie ripped the plastic sheet off a table in the corner, revealing a goblet, a huge quartz point, a carved wooden stick, and a dagger. Kimmie grabbed the dagger, unsheathed it, and whirled around—

—burying it in the side of Maisie's neck.

Maisie half-screamed and half-gurgled as she dropped to the floor.

Blood everywhere.

Blood on the dagger

Blood on Kimmie's hands.

Kimmie dropped the dagger and fell to her knees beside Maisie, who began to wail, a high-pitched keening that pulsed in a familiar rhythm.

"I'm sorry," Kimmie sobbed. "I'm sorry, I'm sorry ...."

✦

"I'm sorry!" Kimmie jerked awake.

She was in her bedroom, with the lavender walls she and her mom had painted last summer. She touched her royal purple comforter and creamy ivory sheets, grounding herself by focusing on the soft cotton beneath her fingertips.

Through the window, the magnolia tree's branches swayed in a gentle breeze, its pale pink buds yet to open.

"I was dreaming," she told herself. "Dreams can't hurt me. Dreams aren't true."

The litany Kimmie's therapist had made her memorize did little to improve her mood, but at least it was something else to focus on while she waited for her heart to stop pounding.

She was awake, but the pulsing wail continued.

Her phone. She grabbed it from the nightstand and answered.

"Are you ready to start the best day of the rest of your life?" April said before Kimmie could manage Hello. "If you come over early, we can get dressed together and—"

Kimmie groaned. "Could we talk about anything else for two seconds?"

A moment of offended silence, then: "What crawled up your butt this morning?"

"I just woke up."

"And?"

Did she want to talk about it? Normally she didn't talk about those dreams to anyone because she didn't want her mom to take her back to the therapist for more pills that made her life feel like a nightmare.

But if she could convince April to change her plans for tonight, it was worth the risk of someone calling her crazy.

"I had a dream. About Maisie. The girl who—"

"I know who Maisie was." There was a long pause, then April asked, "What about Maisie?"

I dreamed I killed her. "About her dying. In that house."

"Is this really about the house? Because I think what you're really nervous about is finally doing it with Noah tonight."

Of course, April would think that. That was all she talked about lately, how she'd been making Spencer wait and how prom night would be The Night. April watched way too many movies.

"Was Noah in the dream?" April added when Kimmie didn't answer.

Kimmie gritted her teeth together. April had a one-track mind when she wanted something. "No, Noah was not in the dream. But Maisie's killer was. I—"

"You can back out with Noah if you want, but you have to keep your promise to me."

"Why can't we just go to prom like everyone else?"

"Nobody's ever managed to make it all night—"

"Alive," Kimmie interrupted. "Maisie's body was there until they found her the next morning."

"Maisie killed herself. You're not suicidal, are you?"

"I heard a serial killer got her."

Or a squatter. Or a drug dealer. Did it matter who did it? She was still dead.

"Look, there's going to be nine of us, and Noah and Spencer are on the football team," April said in her don't argue with me voice. "Ten, if my weirdo brother isn't lying about having a date. No one's going to mess with us."

Kimmie stared out the window at the magnolia tree, still waving its branches in the breeze. The gentle, rhythmic movement made her think of rocking in her mother's chair. Maybe she could pretend to be sick. Stay home and make brownies. Watch movies all night until Mom came home from her graveyard shift at the hospital.

April would be pissed, but she'd get over it. Probably.

"If we make it through the night without freaking out, we'll be legends," April said. "Don't you want to be a legend?"

"I don't get why you care."

"Because you're going away to college in the fall, and you're probably never coming back."

"I'm coming ba—"

"Meanwhile, I'm going to be stuck here in Bellwether with a dumb job, like my mom was." April sniffed. "I'll probably end up being a realtor. And have eight kids. And end up chain-smoking menthols and making art from cigarette butts."

Like always, Kimmie couldn't help laughing.

"Are you really going to deprive me of my last chance at fame in this shithole town?"

"I could take a gap year," Kimmie said like she always did. "We could get our prereqs out of the way at the community college and transfer together."

"I don't know how many times I have to tell you I'm done with school."

But I don't want us to be done. Another thing Kimmie couldn't say to April, not without making things weird. So, she crossed her fingers and changed the topic.

"Is Toby actually bringing a date, or did he buy two tickets so he wouldn't have to stay home?"

"How would I know what that little creep is up to?" April paused, then: "We have to let him come with us; he blackmailed me."

"With what?"

"If I tell everyone, that defeats the purpose of paying the blackmailer."

Great, Toby was going to be there. Another thing about tonight on the suck list. April's fraternal twin had been crushing on Kimmie for as long as she'd been friends with April. He was like a rain cloud that hovered around them every time Kimmie went over there. The worst part was that she couldn't just ask him to stop. He never did anything overtly inappropriate, never hit on her, or tried to get her alone.

Instead, he just … hovered—all the time. He was always watching. Always listening.

He never gave her an opening to say, I'm not interested in dating you.

"Look, you'll be with Noah," April said. "Toby might creep on you from a distance, but ignore him. Everything will be fine."

"Promise?"

"Promise. Tonight will probably be just as boring as you think it will be." April muttered something under her breath: "Gotta go, Grandma's up."

April hung up before Kimmie had a chance to say goodbye.

Kimmie sighed and set her phone back on the nightstand. April was probably right; tonight would be exactly what Kimmie expected.

An awkward dinner with Noah while April and Spencer flirted with each other.

A sweaty gym full of classmates she'd seen practically every day for the last four years, dressed up in clothes they'd only wear once, dancing to music that Kimmie had already heard enough times to be permanently sick of it.

And after prom, a party in a decrepit house, no different from the times they'd gone into the woods to drink and make out. April would insist on doing a Tarot reading for everyone. Spencer would pour shots from a bottle bought by his older brother. Riley would probably sing some weepy Irish thing that her mom taught her before she died, and Zach would tell ghost stories while holding an actual flashlight under his chin because, he would say, it's traditional. Quinn and Brittany would disappear early, pretending to be tired so they could snuggle up together somewhere, too shy to make out in front of everyone else.

The only difference was that Kimmie planned to trust Noah more than she'd ever trusted anyone.

That was scarier than any so-called haunted house.

TWO

Cradling her prom dress, Kimmie entered April's bedroom to find her best friend perched on the edge of the bed in a lacy black bra and panties as she finished putting on jewelry. The charms on her friendship bracelet, a set Kimmie and April shared since fifth grade, quietly tinkled her on her wrist as she then leaned down to fasten a delicate gold-and rhinestone chain around her ankle.

"Do you think Spencer will like it?" April raised a leg to show off her newest accessory.

Stop staring. Kimmie forced herself to focus on the shimmery red prom dress spread out across the bed: a simple sheath with spaghetti straps and a skirt with slits in the sides to reveal a lot of leg. April half-dressed in the school locker room surrounded by thirty other chattering, sweaty girls after phys ed was a lot different than April half-dressed in lingerie, asking for advice on how to make sure that tonight, Spencer would—

"You look amazing," Kimmie said, hating the sudden rush of heat to her cheeks. She'd promised herself that she wouldn't be jealous. Not tonight. "How can he not love it?"

She turned away to close the door in case April wanted to cover up.

Instead, April laughed. "I don't know why you always get so embarrassed. We're both girls, aren't we?"

"I'm not … I just—"

April wasn't embarrassed because, as far as April was concerned, they were just friends. And Kimmie wasn't going to do anything to risk losing that friendship.

"Show me your undies," April demanded, pointing an imperious finger. "You're wearing granny panties again, aren't you?"

Kimmie took a deep breath and held up her dress, the dry-cleaning bag covering it crinkling, hoping to distract April from further thoughts of underwear inspection. "It's not as pretty as yours."

"Once I'm done accessorizing you, you will look stunning. Put it on."

Kimmie turned away and stripped, then held up the simple gown her mother had insisted on buying for her. An A-line with three-quarter sleeves and scoop neck, its midnight blue fabric fell in clean lines that wouldn't be ruined later when Mom shortened the skirt, converting it into something nice that Kimmie could wear for dressy occasions.

But who wants to look nice on prom night? This might be her last big evening with April before she left for college.

The bedroom door opened just as Kimmie started to pull the dress over her head — she yelped, retreating backward and covering herself.

Shit. It was Toby, April's brother, in a powder blue tuxedo that hung on his skinny frame and a paler blue shirt with frilly ruffles running up and down the front. He had slicked back his hair, the same red-gold as April's. It looked like a greasy helmet, more than his usual mad scientist vibe.

Even creepier than usual.

"Jesus, Toby, what about knocking?" April threw a pillow at him, which he dodged like an expert. "Is that Grandpa's tuxedo?"

Toby ignored April, looking near but not quite at Kimmie. Was he being polite? Or was he trying to get a good glimpse without getting caught?

Kimmie clutched the dress against her more tightly.

"Sorry," Toby said. "Spencer and Noah are here with the limo."

"Well, we can't finish getting dressed until you get your creepy ass out of here!" April snapped.

Thankfully, Toby shut the door. Kimmie dressed in seconds, and as she turned around, April gathered up her hair and presented Kimmie with her bare back, pale skin broken only by the satiny black bra straps framed by the edges of the shimmery red sheath dress.

"Zip me up?"

Kimmie's face flushed again, fiery-hot, and she eased the zipper up, trying not to touch April's bare skin.

April grabbed her jewelry box from the bed, and as she walked toward Kimmie for a split-second, Kimmie thought she saw a faint bruise on the outside of her thigh before the fabric closed again. Or maybe it was a shadow.

April held up a delicate pendant — a heart-shaped sapphire surrounded by tiny diamonds — which she fastened around Kimmie's neck.

"It's almost exactly the same color as your dress," she announced with satisfaction, turning her best friend around to face her. April grabbed Kimmie's hands and held them in hers as she beamed a mega-watt smile. Kimmie thought for a second she would faint. "Noah's going to love it."

The bubble burst.

"I don't know." Kimmie's stomach knotted harder with every thought about what she planned to do tonight. "What if it turns out he doesn't like me enough?"

"He does; he's been talking to Spencer for weeks about how he can hardly wait for tonight."

But was that because of her or what they planned to do?

Her face must've given something away because April asked, "You're still okay with Spencer and me, right?"

"I'm happy for both of you," she lied because she wasn't letting Spencer take April away from her. April would give him what Kimmie wouldn't — sex — and then they'd get bored with each other. And everything would go back to normal. "If you're happy, I'm happy."

April hugged Kimmie and gave her hand a reassuring squeeze. "Trust me; tonight will be amazing."

Kimmie squeezed back and nodded. No matter what happened, it would be happening to them both.

As long as they were together, everything would be okay.

◆

Toby hung back in the dining room, fidgeting with his Rubik's cube while his sister and Kimmie crowded together with their dates in front of the living room fireplace. Kimmie took his breath away — her elegant dark blue dress was a million times classier than April's garish outfit, in that shade of red showing the maximum amount of skin that Grandmother would allow. Like everything April wore, it screamed look at me! Most people wouldn't notice the sweet but infinitely more sophisticated Kimmie standing beside her.

But Toby did.

And Noah, who'd asked her out five seconds after Spencer had broken up with her.

Totally ruining Toby's plans.

Noah seemed like a decent guy, but being best friends with Spencer proved otherwise. Spencer was everything that was wrong with high school. He was a good-looking jock who used other people to gratify his ego, then discarded them when they didn't do what he wanted. When he met someone he didn't have a use for, he tormented them verbally. And everyone loved him for it.

Noah went along with whatever Spencer did, which made him just as bad.

Kimmie deserved so much better than someone like Spencer or Noah. Even Toby's slutty sister, April, deserved better. Yet both of them cared more about the football players' good looks than about their characters.

"Toby, why don't we take some pictures with you?" his grandmother said.

"Yeah, Toby, don't you want to document the night of your most epic date ever?" Spencer chimed in.

Asshole.

"That's okay," Toby said. "There'll be a photographer at prom. Jenny and I will take pictures there."

Everyone looked skeptical; he didn't care. He'd had to ask someone — you couldn't go to prom alone. And there was no way he'd miss the chance to ask Kimmie to dance.

As a friend, of course, because she was there with Noah, this would still be his chance to let her know how he felt.

Jenny had already said she didn't mind as long as she got to go with them to the haunted house afterward.

Toby stared at Grandpa Warren, who sat at the dining room table and stared at his untouched food, a string of drool hanging from the corner of his mouth. Toby hadn't much liked Grandpa Warren before the stroke — the old man had been jealous of the attention Grandma Patricia lavished on Toby, which he criticized as coddling that would keep Toby from growing up to be a man.

Toby liked Grandpa Warren much better after the stroke.

"I'd like to take some pictures of my handsome grandson," Grandma said to Toby. Then she added, "You look perfect in your grandfather's tuxedo. You know, I dated him in high school before he married that woman. I never doubted that he'd come back to me, and he did."

Toby nodded, not wanting to get Grandma started, not in front of Kimmie. "Okay, just a couple of pictures."

At least he could stand next to Kimmie. When he helped Grandma upload them, he would crop the others out, and have a real picture of them together.

He set his Rubik's cube down on the table.

Spencer said, "Don't forget to hold up the corsage you got your date."

But when Toby approached the others in front of the fireplace, they didn't just scoot over to make room for him. Spencer led the four of them into the dining room, leaving Toby standing all alone.

"That's my handsome boy," Grandma said as he smiled for the camera.

"That's her handsome boy," Spencer echoed, elbowing Noah while Kimmie and April whispered to each other.

Asshole.

❖

Click.

Click.

Click.

Kimmie tried to ignore the sound of Toby twisting his Rubik's cube into new configurations. But as irritating as it was, he preferred it to seeing Spencer and April trying to suck each other's faces off in the back seat of the limo Spencer's dad had rented for them.

Or maybe it was the smell that was bothering her. The pine-scented air freshener barely covered up the ghosts of cigarette smoke, spilled champagne, and vomit, all mixed in with the musky cologne that

Spencer must've showered in before donning that expensive tuxedo. That made him look extremely hot. Or should have.

Really, he looked like he was trying too hard.

Noah had worn nice slacks and a sport coat — because you're the gem, and I'm the setting, he'd whispered while April's grandmother took pictures of them. He put his arm around her shoulders and pulled her closer, but she was already too hot.

Kimmie's stomach lurched.

"Are you feeling carsick?"

Toby had stopped playing with his puzzle cube to stare at her like he was afraid she'd faint.

"If you're not used to sitting sideways, it messes with your inner ear," he added. "I don't mind trading seats if you want."

"She's fine here with me." Noah was practically crushing her against him.

"I want to switch." She unlatched her seatbelt and scooted forward, out from under his arm, and turned to face him. "I think I am carsick."

Noah hesitated for a moment, shooting an annoyed look at Toby. But then he smiled. "Sure, whatever you want."

"Ow!" Spencer detached himself from April to glare at Kimmie as she settled into the seat facing them. "You stepped on my foot."

"Sorry." She hadn't meant to step on him. But as hard as it was to watch her best friend make out with her ex, it was harder to pretend it didn't hurt that he'd dumped her for her best friend. So, her sorry leaned a little toward not sorry.

"It's not her fault; you're so tall, you're taking up half the limo," Toby said, defending Kimmie even though she didn't want him to.

But she hated Spencer's smug expression even more than she was creeped out by Toby's weird concern for her.

"Where's your date again?" Spencer pulled a flask out of his jacket pocket and offered it to April. She grinned and took a sip.

"I'm meeting her there." Click. Click. Click.

"Weird that we haven't met her."

"He says she's doing all independent study classes," April said.

"So, she doesn't live in Canada?" Spencer pushed.

"We believe you, buddy." That was Noah, always the hero, at least when everyone was watching. But Kimmie wondered what he would be like tonight when they were finally alone.

Click. Click. Click.

April offered Kimmie the flask, but she shook her head — she wanted to get out of this stuffy limo and into the dance, where she could pull April away from Spencer for a few minutes.

"There's more where that came from," Spencer said as Noah took another sip and passed the flask. "My brother stashed a fifth of vodka at the Bain house. For later."

Kimmie didn't want to think about later. Right now was hard enough. The limo was hot and stuffy, and Spencer's cologne was scrubbing the back of her throat raw. No matter how little air she took in, her stomach kept getting queasier.

Finally, she saw the lighted sign. Bellwether High School.

The limo's partition slid down with a faint grinding noise.

"I'm going to be back here at eleven," the driver said as he pulled the car up to the curb. "If I have to come in looking for you kids, I'm charging your parents extra."

Kimmie scrambled out of the car, her long skirt tangling with her legs as she straightened, almost tripping her. But April caught her elbow and kept her from falling — and suddenly, she could breathe again.

"Dance with me, at least once," she blurted.

"This is prom," April said, taking Spencer's arm. "We'll be dancing together all night."

Not the same.

THREE

As Noah guided Kimmie into the gym, she inched closer to him — more to get farther from Toby, who'd decided to walk on her other side as if he was her other date. Even more embarrassing, he still carried the Rubik's cube, tossing it from one hand to the other and occasionally making another move.

So, she turned her back to him as if admiring the prom committee's work. They'd started with Under the Sea, and the decorations were exactly what Kimmie expected: metallic blue-green tinsel curtains, a castle sculpted from kinetic sand on the table near the door, sand dollars, and starfishes everywhere. Light projectors cast watery blue light on the walls and ceilings, and a bubble machine behind the dais at the far end of the gym blew a steady stream of bubbles that floated over the dance floor.

Half the girls wore gowns with mermaid-style skirts, and Rufus from Kimmie's homeroom was cosplaying a shirtless Aquaman with fake tattoos drawn in permanent marker.

But Kimmie couldn't stop staring at the DJ, dressed in a 70's-style neon green pantsuit and a rubber Cthulhu mask. He danced like he was being electrocuted in time with the music. A small cluster of boys near the dais — probably on the football team and definitely drunk — mimicked the DJ's every move, howling and roaring at who knew what.

DJ Cthulhu pointed at his mockers and attempted a move that involved a lot of pelvic thrusts and kung fu punches at the ceiling.

"Is he dancing like nobody's watching or having a seizure?"

April laughed at Spencer's joke. "Wait, didn't Mr. Macklin volunteer to DJ this year?"

"Trust the chemistry teacher to have access to the good stuff," Noah added.

Kimmie caught sight of Zach and Riley, headed straight for them — Zach in black jeans and a T-shirt with the outlines of a tuxedo printed on it, Riley in a thrift store dress that looked right out of Little House on the Prairie, stiletto boots, and a studded leather collar with a big silver ring attached to a chain that dangled down between her breasts.

"This is even more hilariously stupid than I thought it would be," Riley announced as she hugged Kimmie.

Zach grinned. "Anyone want a taste of Cinderella's Dream?"

Kimmie turned to April. "What does that mean?"

"Weed." April tugged on Spencer's arm. "Want."

"Me too," Noah added.

Toby muttered something that sounded a lot like grandma said not to.

Apparently, Spencer heard. "You weren't invited, dork."

April punched Spencer in the arm. "He's still my brother."

But then she turned to Toby. "You aren't invited, and if you tell anyone, I'll tell too."

Toby flushed and walked away.

"Problem solved," April announced. "You coming, Kimmie?"

"Not yet." Not at all, but she was tired of being called the group's goody-two-shoes. "I want to say hi to Quinn and Brittany."

April smiled — looking a little disappointed. — and left with Spencer.

Riley pointed to the dance floor, and Kimmie couldn't believe she hadn't noticed them. Quinn, dressed in a three-piece suit and fedora, like a mobster in an old movie, and Brittany, who could have been Mae West back from the dead in a curve-hugging gown and a wavy bob. While everyone else gyrated around them, they were ballroom dancing, holding each other close, never breaking eye contact. They looked so ... in love.

Kimmie would give anything to dance with April like that.

✦

April couldn't hold it in any longer. She coughed out the musky, citrusy smoke as everyone else laughed.

Spencer held the joint out to her again. "One more time?"

"Give it a chance to hit," Riley said, snatching it away from him and patting April on the back. "You're doing great. Just breathe."

Was it hitting? She couldn't feel anything yet. Just the burning in her lungs and the tear wetting her cheek as she coughed again.

"Hey, remember Denny's?" Zach said, and everyone else laughed again.

April laughed too, but a second too late.

"Spencer just about pissed his pants when Coach Katz came around that corner." Brittany snort-laughed like it was the funniest thing she'd ever heard.

Brittany could laugh like that and not get teased because she was gorgeous and on the cheerleading squad. April had laughed like that once in third grade, and for the rest of the year, Brandy and Misha had called her pig-girl.

"I told him Coach wasn't going to bench his best quarterback for a little weed," Noah said. "But did he believe me?"

April couldn't help but feel jealous as they reminisced about The Breakdown, which they talked about like it was some epic thing when really, it was just sharing a joint after an away game while waiting for a tow truck driver to give their old bus a jump start.

Noah and Spencer were always talking about games, and since Brittany was a cheerleader and Zach and Riley were in the marching band, they were usually there to witness the shenanigans.

April hated being on the outside of an inside joke.

But she and Kimmie had become part of the group at the beginning of the year when Spencer had asked Kimmie out. If Spencer hadn't wanted to date April next, would the others have still wanted them in the group? Or would they have sided with Spencer against Kimmie, kicking April out because she was Kimmie's best friend?

She was glad she'd never had to find out.

Now that high school was practically over, all that mattered was tonight. And graduation. And the fun they'd have until summer was over and everyone went away to college.

She had to make sure that tonight was perfect for both herself and Kimmie.

So, she turned to Noah and said, "Isn't Kimmie adorable tonight?"

"You should've seen her watch Quinn and Brittany dance," Zach butted in. "I think she wants in on that action."

Did he have to turn everything into something sexual? "Stop it. She's totally into Noah. She's just ... nervous."

Zach turned to Riley as if something serious had just occurred to him. "If Quinn and Brittany invite me to a threesome tonight, I'm going to have to honor that request. You understand, right?"

"Since when are we doing threesomes?" Riley asked.

"Since you said you thought Rufus was hot as Aquaman."

"I only said that because you were ogling Samantha Mackenzie's cleavage."

"It was exceptionally fine cleavage."

Riley slapped Zach on the chest. "I hate you sometimes."

"But you love me more times." He grabbed Riley by the waist and gave her a sloppy kiss. Which turned into an impromptu make-out session.

Ugh. Why wasn't she feeling anything yet? The clock was ticking on her perfect prom night, and here she was, standing in the shadows so a chaperone wouldn't see them, waiting for Zach's weak ass weed to kick in.

Noah had the joint. She held out her hand. "If I have to watch this, I will need another hit."

"You sure?" Noah asked. "It can take a few minutes to start feeling it."

"The lady said she wants another hit." Spencer took the joint from Noah and handed it to April. "Whatever she wants tonight, she gets."

As she took another drag, April wished Kimmie had come outside with them. The world felt a little bit wobbly right now, and it wasn't just the weed. Graduation was right around the corner, and Kimmie planned to go to college, leaving April here to work some dumb job so she could move out into her own place. Spencer was good enough to be her first time, but he wasn't The One, and April was starting to worry that maybe there never would be One for her.

More and more, she felt like she had no control over who she was becoming or what her life would be like.

But even though Kimmie revolved around April, somehow, she was the stable one. She seemed unaffected by all the pressure to be smart, pretty, and popular. She hadn't changed much at all since they'd first sat next to each other in fifth grade, and April had told her, we're friends now.

Things never got out of control when Kimmie was around.

Kimmie's heart raced as she swayed with Noah, taking tiny steps, staring at the red rose boutonnière. He was the same Noah she'd hung out with every day at school — at lunch, parties, and at football games. But when he smiled at her now, standing so close with his hand on her waist, it felt so ... intimate should've been the right word, but invasive was closer to the truth.

She shivered, thinking about what would happen after prom. Her first time. She'd said yes to him because he'd always been nice to her, even when she was dating Spencer. But that intense look on his face made her wonder if she'd made a mistake. Why wasn't she glowing the way April glowed when Spencer looked at her like that?

Someone tapped Noah on the shoulder. "May I cut in?"

He looked annoyed as he turned, but it was only Quinn, minus her fedora. And minus Brittany, too.

"Yes," said Kimmie, trying not to sound relieved.

Noah looked even more annoyed. "I'll get us some punch."

Quinn offered her hand to Kimmie, like in an old movie, but when Kimmie took it, she was led off to a dark corner. Where Brittany sat at a small table, the missing fedora on her head.

"You don't have to do it if you don't want to." Quinn pulled a seat out for Kimmie. "If Noah's pressuring you—"

"I want to," Kimmie said quickly. "I'm fine."

Quinn and Brittany traded a look as Kimmie sat.

"When are you going to tell her how you feel?" Brittany asked.

"Tell who what?"

"It's obvious you're in love with April."

Kimmie hoped it was dark enough that no one could see how hard she was blushing.

"It's obvious to us," Quinn added. "The guys don't have a clue."

Brittany nodded dramatically. "Especially Noah."

"April and I are friends. Best friends. That's how I feel about her."

"But if she knew you were interested—"

"She's with Spencer." But what if that was the reason Spencer had decided to date April? What if he could tell Kimmie loved April, and he'd wanted to punish her for refusing to—

"Would she be if she knew?" Brittany asked.

"I'd rather be friends." And right now, Kimmie would rather be hanging with April, even if it meant letting Noah get uncomfortably close and putting up with Spencer's attitude. Was April still outside? How long did it take to get high anyway? It happened right away when people smoked on TV. "Where is she?"

"Sometimes telling a person how you feel doesn't ruin the friendship." Quinn stood and pulled Brittany to her feet. "Sometimes it makes the friendship better."

Brittany giggled as Quinn spun her around and dipped her, diving in for a quick kiss.

Kimmie couldn't help being jealous of how in synch they were. They had the same interests, same dreams, and they were even going to the same college. There didn't seem to be a single thing that they didn't love about each other.

"I'm going to find—" Kimmie caught a flash of red out of the corner of her eye on the other side of the gym, near the door that led to the locker rooms.

"Tell Noah I'll be right back."

FOUR

A few minutes later, Kimmie broke through the line of couples waiting to have their pictures taken in front of the Atlantis mural art students had painted on plywood and erected under the basketball hoop. A marble arch, with fallen columns in the background, colorful fish darting through the surrounding water, and an octopus was waving in the corner. So corny.

Kimmie hustled into the hallway and turned sharp right—

—and screamed as she stared into the open jaws of a massive great white shark.

Someone grabbed her from behind, a strong arm looping around her waist.

"It's okay," Noah said, pulling her back against him. "It's just papier-mâché."

Kimmie shuddered, forcing herself to take a deep breath as she studied the sculpture — suspended from the ceiling with clear fishing wire. Obvious now that she knew what to look for. But in the dim light, it had seemed terrifyingly real.

"Where were you going, Kimmie?"

"I thought I saw April—"

"She's with Spencer."

"Where?"

Noah hesitated, letting her go before he answered. "I'm not sure they want company right now."

Maybe that was true, but she'd rather hear that from April herself.

Kimmie hurried down the hallway, leaving Noah behind as she slammed through the girl's locker room door.

"Hey!" Noah yelled, but he didn't follow her in.

Kimmie groped for the light switch, squinting as the fluorescents flickered to life. She checked showers, the toilets, and even the coach's office—no April.

When she emerged, Noah was waiting. "I told you, you don't want—"

"Do you know where they went?"

Noah's eyes slid left toward the door that led outside. Kimmie pushed it open, revealing Spencer sitting on a bench, April on his lap, the straps of her dress far enough down her shoulders that the bodice had to be partially unzipped.

April turned her head to stare glassily at Kimmie, eyes too wide, smile too bright. "Hey!"

Now she understood why Noah hadn't wanted her to keep looking. But she held her ground, despite the growing heat in her face. April didn't look wasted more than happy. If Kimmie left April with Spencer now, would April regret trusting him tomorrow?

"Are you …" Maybe Kimmie was crossing a line, but … "You've been gone so long, I was wondering if you were okay."

"We're fine!" Spencer snapped.

"Kimmie thought she saw a chaperone headed your way and wanted to warn you."

She could've hugged Noah for the save. Why had she been worried about him? He was the only person tonight who hadn't sniped at her, creeped on her, or poked a nose into her business.

"What would Grandmother think?" A new voice asked.

Toby seemed to have emerged from the shadows — and to be holding one of those shadows by its hand. No, it was a girl Kimmie had never seen before, a goth fairy in black and bubblegum pink. Black lace corset with pink ribbon, sheer black floor-length skirt over pink leggings, fingerless black elbow gloves with polished pink nails, and pink high-tops. Even her makeup fit the theme, shimmery black eyeshadow highlighted in the same pink that tinged her cheeks and lips.

From a black leather cord around her neck hung the weirdest pendant Kimmie had ever seen: a huge silver disk with a circle containing an eight-pointed star inscribed on it, tons of squiggly writing around the edge of the circle, and more squiggly symbols in each of the star's points. At the center was a dark red cabochon, like a big shiny drop of blood turned to stone.

"Shut up, Toby." April struggled to her feet, almost losing her balance until her hand caught Spencer's shoulder. "My mouth is so dry."

Kimmie held a hand out to her friend. "Let's get some punch."

April beamed and hooked her arm through Kimmie's. But as she did, her dress started to slide down.

"Uh …" Noah started.

"Slut," Toby whispered. "You'll be in so much trouble when Grandma finds out."

"If you tell her, you can't come with us after," April reminded him dreamily. "You'll have to find another haunted house for your date."

Toby's lips tightened, but he took Jenny's hand and led her to the dance floor.

Kimmie slipped behind April and zipped her back up, then tugged her shoulder straps back into place.

April whirled and grabbed her, hugging her tight.

"I love you so much, Kimmie."

I love you too.

But she wasn't going to say it while Spencer watched with that sour look on his face. Besides, she wasn't sure if April would have said it sober, and how embarrassing would it be tomorrow if April didn't mean it the way Kimmie did?

So, she settled for, "You're my best friend."

It was better than nothing.

✦

Noah watched as Kimmie zipped April's dress back up and hugged her, then linked arms and led her friend onto the dance floor. April started to shimmy provocatively, then Kimmie said something, and they both dissolved into giggles.

Noah turned to Spencer and frowned. "Out in the quad, where anyone could've walked by?"

"But nobody did walk by until Kimmie came looking. It's like they're attached at the hip."

"She's nervous about later. Give her a break."

"Or she's still mad that I dumped her, and she's getting her revenge by cock-blocking me with April."

"Chill, dude," Noah said. "You're going to have all night with April."

For some reason, that made Spencer look sad.

"Hey, I got you something." He fished a small object out of his pocket and held it out to Noah.

Noah took it and held it up so that one of the colored lights illuminated it as it moved past.

"A toy car?" he asked.

"The Porsche 911 GT3 you've been talking about," Spencer replied. "For until you get drafted for the NFL and can afford a real one."

Noah laughed and fist-bumped Spencer. "Thanks, man. You want to—"

"Your friendship has been the best thing about this year."

"I'm going to miss you too."

"No, I mean it."

Spencer shifted from one foot to the other. Noah had never seen him look nervous before. What was this?

"I know we're both going to be busy," Spencer said, "but I hope we can keep in touch. Hang out on the holidays."

"Yeah, sure."

Then Spencer launched himself at Noah, embracing him in an almost crushing hug. "Hey, it's just college. I'm not dying."

"You're the best." Spencer slapped him on the back hard, as if that would make this not weird. "I love you, man."

The weed they'd smoked had been strong, but not that strong. Noah extricated himself from the hug and squinted at his friend. "How much of that vodka did you drink?"

Spencer blinked hard, reached into his jacket and pulled out the flask. "Not enough."

Noah grabbed it from him and tucked it into his lapel pocket. The prom committee hadn't thought to include coffee with the refreshments, so he needed another way to sober Spencer up.

"The girls are resorting to dancing with themselves," he said. "Let's not leave them hanging."

As he turned toward Kimmie, Spencer grumbled something that could've been, what about leaving me hanging?

Noah decided to ignore it.

◆

April felt the weed more intensely than she'd ever felt it before. It was making her light-headed in a warm, happy way, making her skin tingle and muscles loose and relaxed, and turning up the colors on everything around her. She felt like she could dance forever. And she wanted to hug everyone.

Everyone except Toby, who was being a jerk like usual. And Toby's creepy date. They'd disappeared as Kimmie had led April to the dance floor, arms linked like Kimmie was her date.

April put her hands in the air like she didn't care because DJ Cthulhu's corny old song told her to, but she cared so much. About all of them. As she swung her hips in time to the music, she watched her friends dance together — maybe for the last time ever.

Riley and Zach took turns grinding on each other to the funky beat with enthusiasm. Riley's cheeks were flushed as she laughed at the silly face Zach made as he randomly switched to the robot for no apparent reason. Riley was so pretty; she'd be one of the most popular girls in school, if only she weren't so weird. But she seemed perfectly happy to date a goofy stoner. April couldn't help but wonder what it would be like to not care what other people thought. Sometimes she was even a tiny bit jealous of how carefree Riley seemed.

Quinn and Brittany were in their own little world too, so in synch that April wondered how much time they'd spent practicing just for prom. They'd switched from ballroom-style to modern, and they were so good, could've been shooting a TikTok video. April had been there the day they'd met in drama class, freshman year, and she'd known they were meant for each other even before Quinn had chosen Brittany to play the balcony scene from Romeo and Juliet with her. The two of them were so lucky — they'd both made it into the same college, so things wouldn't change hardly at all for them.

Sometimes, she wished Spencer would look at her like Quinn looked at Brittany.

Not that the way he looked at her was bad. And the fact that he was looking at her at all made her the most-envied girl at school, if not the most popular. He would've been the hottest guy at school, even if he wasn't the best quarterback Bellwether had ever had, leading them to the division championship for the past three years.

Kimmie had felt uncomfortable being the focus of so much jealousy, but April loved it when the cheerleaders, the rich girls, and even the cutest of the nerds glared at her for monopolizing the cutest guy in school. Before Spencer, April had been the girl who shopped at the thrift store with her allowance because she didn't want to wear the clothes her grandmother made her. She'd become marginally more interesting when she'd started doing Tarot readings at lunch, with big gold hoops dangling from her ears and a secondhand scarf tied through her hair. Catching Spencer's attention had been a total shock —an opportunity that no sane girl would turn down.

Except for Kimmie.

Kimmie hadn't been able to handle Spencer's intensity, not like April could. She needed a nice boyfriend, someone who would respect her boundaries and take things slow and gently. Someone boring, like Noah.

As the funk shifted to upbeat pop, April glanced at her best friend, who was doing a boring side-to-side shuffle in time with Noah.

Noah danced like the song was a pop quiz, and he'd just woken up at school in his underwear.

Kimmie noticed April watching and smiled back, the sweetest smile. April's heart beat faster. She loved her best friend so much. Kimmie was the first person who'd ever really cared about April. More than April's mother before she'd died. Much more than April's brother Toby, who was supposed to watch out for her as the older twin by three minutes. Even more than Spencer, who could hardly wait to be April's first lover.

She loved Kimmie so much that when she'd hugged her, it had been hard to let her go. She could've hugged short, soft, sweet Kimmie all night. Kimmie's hands had felt warm through the thin, shimmery fabric of April's dress. And Kimmie's hair smelled like lavender and vanilla and something else, something that might've been her conditioner or maybe just been Kimmie. That scent made her feel relaxed and happy, and safe. She'd almost kissed the side of Kimmie's neck.

But that must have been the weed — she'd never been this high before, so high she was practically floating, like the bubbles drifting down over the dance floor. Her bubble would pop later when Kimmie and Spencer, and everyone else went away to college, leaving April behind, feeling like a loser.

But tonight, April's life was perfect.

✦

The music was playing, a thumping dance beat, but one of those lapses in conversation happened for no apparent reason. Toby glanced at the metal-caged clock on the gym wall: twenty minutes after the hour, precisely what he'd expected. It always seemed to be twenty after the hour when the conversations bouncing around the table suddenly died.

His grandmother always said that it was because twenty minutes after the hour was the time when angels in heaven would sing, and everyone, unconsciously or not, would pause to listen. A cute idea.

His grandfather's explanation made more sense: We're just monkeys that have evolved to shut up after talking for twenty minutes. So, we can listen for predators.

Like Spencer. He was a predator, an animal. What he'd done to April tonight proved it. Why were women so often blind to the fact that Spencer and guys like him were just looking to take advantage of them?

It was, he supposed, one of the things that made them so attractive. Their vulnerability. Their weakness. They got themselves into trouble so men like him could rescue them. Damsels in distress, all of them. Every girl wanted to be a fairy tale princess, getting saved from a dragon.

Did killing dragons make you a predator? No, it wasn't the same thing. When a knight slays a dragon, he does it for love.

"Is everyone sick of dancing?" Kimmie broke the lull in the conversation. That was the opening Toby had been looking for all night — the chance to get Kimmie away from Noah without seeming like he was butting in.

He popped up and circled the table. "I haven't danced with you yet." He offered his hand with a slight bow. "Would you be so kind as to do me the honor?"

Kimmie looked around the table, but everyone else was still spacing out, thanks to Zach's weed and Spencer's little flask. Kimmie was the only one who'd resisted the temptation to dull her mind. Another thing he loved about her.

"Sure, why not," she said, standing up awkwardly.

He gestured, "After you," and gently placed his fingertips at the small of her back, guiding her through the scattered tables and chairs to the dance floor.

They started dancing in place, a few feet apart, Kimmie looking right and left and occasionally at Toby with a lopsided grin.

"You're a good dancer!" Toby yelled to be heard over the music. He wanted her to feel appreciated.

"I never know what to do with my hands!" shouted Kimmie. "April's so much better at it than me."

The song would be over soon—time to get serious. Toby leaned forward so his mouth was near her ear. "Aren't you worried about Noah?"

Kimmie stopped dancing for a beat. "What?"

Toby bounced forward again. "Noah. Aren't you worried about him? You know, because of Spencer?"

The music shifted abruptly—slow dance.

Kimmie hesitated. Before she could make an excuse and run back to Noah, Toby stepped forward and put his hand on her waist.

Then he whispered in her ear. "Spencer was trying to rape April."

Kimmie followed Toby as he swayed slowly to the music, but she kept him at arm's length rather than plastering herself against him. He respected that. "Spencer was being a jerk, Toby, but he's not a rapist. Things just got a little out of hand."

"What would have happened if you hadn't been there to break things up?"

"I don't know ... It doesn't matter, I was there, and that's what counts. End of story."

"Noah spends a lot of time with Spencer, doesn't he?"

"So?" Kimmie was defensive.

Toby sighed inwardly. Princesses and dragons, he reminded himself. "Don't you ever worry that Spencer's whole rapey vibe is rubbing off on Noah?"

"Toby, don't be a shit."

"I'm just trying to open your eyes, Kimmie. Guys like Spencer and Noah are on the prowl. They're animals, and the sooner you realize it the better."

Kimmie scoffed. "You sound jealous."

That was the power of dragons. So often, the damsel in distress was complicit in her abuse. He knew that women were just blind to these things, but sometimes they almost seemed to be into it.

But if he had to be mad at anyone, it was the dragons not the damsels in this world.

"You are an amazing woman, Kimmie. I would kill for you. If anyone ever hurts you, you call me." His heart beat heavily in his chest, and he was afraid she would feel it. "Call me, and I will be there to do whatever you need."

He let the words hang in the air between them. There, he had finally said it. He had basically just told her; I love you. Whether she was smart enough to understand that remained to be seen, but the important thing was that somewhere, on some basic, instinctive level, she understood that he was claiming her, that she was his.

"I, uh, thanks for the dance, Toby." She broke away, grabbing his arm by the wrist and pushing it away from her.

She headed quickly back to the table with the rest of them.

Toby followed at a leisurely pace. He knew love was a lot to take in. Give her time. But not too much.

◆

Kimmie shifted in her chair so that April could lean her head on Kimmie's shoulder. She seemed entranced by the laser lights strobing in time to DJ Cthulhu's thumping techno groove. April's hair tickled Kimmie's neck. She breathed in the sweet lavender scent of the conditioner that April had used since seventh grade.

Everyone else wanted to talk about what would happen next. But Kimmie wanted to stay here forever.

"Toby said we're going to the Bain house after," Jenny announced. "I can hardly wait to see what it's like inside."

Spencer snorted. "It's like an abandoned house. Because that's what it is."

"A haunted house," Riley warbled in a ghostly voice.

"I'm going to haunt your house." Zach grabbed the chain hanging from Riley's collar and tugged her close enough for a kiss, which immediately turned sloppy.

Noah rolled his eyes. "Get a fucking room, would you."

"Isn't that why we're going there?" Quinn winked at Brittany.

"I thought we were going to meet the ghost," Jenny said, and it sounded like a challenge to Kimmie.

Toby leaned back in his chair, click click clicking his Rubik's cube into new configurations.

But every time he looked up, it seemed like his eyes were on Kimmie. Not Jenny, his date. Or April, his sister. Or even Spencer, who'd been needling him all evening.

"No such thing as ghosts," Quinn said.

"But it's a beautifully tragic story," Brittany said. "Sheila Bain moves here for love, finds out that her husband is cheating on her with his high school sweetheart, and drowns herself out of grief."

Zach stopped necking with Riley long enough to say, "As a psychic, you'd think she'd have known that was going to happen."

"Psychics aren't real," said Riley.

"They are real," April murmured, so soft that Kimmie might've been the only one to hear.

Jenny sounded so sure. Kimmie wondered what she hoped Sheila would say.

"Last dance!" DJ Cthulhu screamed to the gym ceiling. "I wanna see all of you mofos on the dance floor!"

"Someone's getting fired tomorrow," Zach said.

"More like mandatory rehab," Riley countered.

"That's our cue." Spencer stood. "Time for shit to get real."

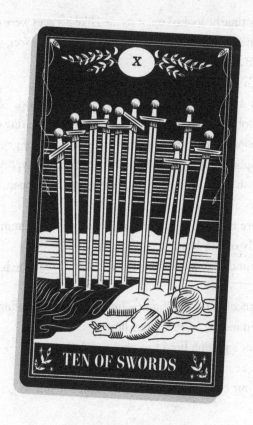

TEN OF SWORDS

FIVE

Kimmie waited on the sidewalk while everyone piled into the limo. Spencer first — he claimed the back seat, pulling April onto his lap. There was just enough room for Riley to sit next to April and Spencer, while Zach grabbed the spot closest to her on the sideways-facing bench.

Toby and Jenny claimed the rest of that one, leaving Noah, Quinn, and Brittany in the seats facing the back window.

"Nine seats, ten people." Spencer shot an annoyed look at Toby, who'd clearly messed up the plan by inviting a date to prom who had actually shown up.

"I can sit on the floor," Kimmie offered as she clambered in.

But before she could arrange her skirt to allow her to sit, strong hands pulled her backward. She fell onto Noah's lap.

"I'll be a gentleman, I promise," he whispered in her ear.

April looked like she approved, but Kimmie felt ... manipulated. Like her best friend was conspiring with the boys to make sure that Kimmie lost her virginity, and she didn't trust Kimmie to follow through on the plan.

It's not April's fault that you got in the car last. Or that Jenny actually showed up. Or that this limo has nine seats.

Spencer twisted to put his seatbelt on, and when his elbow nudged April's leg, she hissed in pain.

"What, babe?"

"Nothing, just a bruise," April said.

"How did you get it?" Kimmie asked. "And the one on your thigh?"

April needed to change the subject. "I brought my Tarot deck. Who wants a reading tonight?"

"I've got something better."

All eyes turned to Jenny, who pretended not to notice the attention as she leaned against Toby, who didn't seem to know what to do about her sudden proximity.

"Nothing's better than Tarot cards." April's imperiousness was back. Kimmie wondered if Jenny was clueless or if she realized she was challenging April's position as the group's resident psychic.

"You can't use Tarot cards to talk to a ghost," Jenny said.

It was a challenge, then.

"No such thing as ghosts." Spencer dismissed her.

Kimmie doubted that Spencer had said it to stick up for April. It hadn't worked if so. Now April looked annoyed with him too.

"Just because you can't explain a psychic phenomenon doesn't mean it's not real."

The limo took a speed bump too fast, and Kimmie's stomach lurched — but she didn't fly off Noah's lap, thanks to his arm around her stomach.

"Sheila Bain was a badass psychic," April announced. "If anyone could come back as a ghost, it would be her."

Jenny nodded like April had said something profound. "To summon a ghost, there's a ritual. I've brought everything we'll need for the spell."

"Are you a witch or something?" Riley asked.

"No such thing as witches either," Spencer grumbled. "I'd like to remind everyone that we already have a plan for tonight."

"Several plans."

April counted them off on her fingers.

"First, the readings. Second, we party. Third, we become legends for lasting the whole night in that house."

"A friend of my brother's said he spent the night there two years ago, and nothing happened."

"Your brother's friend is a liar," April said to Noah.

"Someone did kill Maisie," Riley pointed out. "They found her real body, stabbed with a real knife."

"My cousin said she got so creeped out; she lost it. That she was trying to kill her friends." Brittany's cousin had been there the night that Maisie died. But if Maisie had been that scared, why hadn't she just left?

"I heard your cousin and the others locked Maisie in the house," said Jenny.

"They didn't!" Brittany snapped.

Riley sobered. "My aunt was working in the ER the night they came in. She said they were seriously wasted. And that Maisie probably overdid it and had a psychotic break. That's why she attacked them."

Toby suggested that Maisie had been bitten by a rabid animal hiding in the house, but Kimmie didn't think rabies worked like that.

"Sheriff said she was killed by a squatter and that he was the one who scared them all." Spencer clearly considered the official answer to be the truth. "Maisie just didn't run as fast as the others."

"They never found the squatter. Or the knife." Jenny said, and there was a hint of anger in her voice that didn't match her light-hearted expression.

Spencer shrugged. "He probably took the murder weapon with him. Wouldn't you?"

"I heard her little sister was found with the body," April said. "That she was catatonic, and they had to put her in a psych ward."

"Wasn't she adopted?" Riley asked.

"I heard that too but why does that matter?" said Brittany.

"It doesn't," Quinn said. "It would scar you to find a stranger's dead body."

Dead silence. Then Riley said tentatively: "Are we sure we want to do this?"

"If something bad happens, we'll leave." Zach nuzzled Riley's neck. "We're not idiots, like the teens in every horror movie ever."

"Nothing's going to happen that we don't make happen," said Spencer with finality.

Noah's arm tightened around Kimmie's waist, but he didn't try anything else — no nuzzling, no kissing, just the warmth of his breath on the side of her neck. She felt safe and protected.

He had her, and he wouldn't let her fall, no matter how bumpy the ride got.

Maybe tonight would be fun after all.

◆

The Bain House, a crumbling brick three-story, sat back in a nestle of trees, the front walk having long since been overgrown by oleander bushes. Dead ivy clung to the walls, hanging over the windows on each floor. Its wide porch was lined with once-white columns, now speckled with mold, supporting a widow's walk on the second story that ran the width of the house. Behind the house was the edge of the forest than ran between Bellwether and Shady Vale.

"This house been empty since what? The nineties?" Spencer asked. "But the windows are all still there."

Kimmie ignored the chill in the pit of her stomach. "So?"

Spencer shrugged, and the plastic bags he carried crinkled with the rise of his shoulders. "So, no kids have come up here with a slingshot and a pile of rocks?"

"There's no graffiti either." Riley took a step back. "Why does it feel like this place is watching us?"

Toby's voice was a whisper as he stared at the filthy windows. "I think we should go."

"And do what? Go home?" April scoffed. "No way. We came here to celebrate the end of our senior year, and that's what we're going to do."

"Yeah," Noah said as he stepped up onto the porch.

They picked their way through the overgrown yard, stepping over fallen branches and around tufts of weeds. The closer they got to the house, the more Kimmie's unease seemed to grow. There was something about how it loomed in the darkness, silent and foreboding, making her skin crawl.

And that weird buzzing in her head was back.

Something cold splatted against the side of her neck, and she startled.

Noah grabbed her hand and squeezed it. "I won't let anything happen to you."

She wanted to believe Noah. But she couldn't stop thinking about her nightmare — Maisie chasing her with murderous eyes, the flash of the knife, blood everywhere, and the sound of her own screams echoing through the darkness.

Another icy splat, this time on her collarbone. A raindrop. Perfect, a storm to make their stay in a haunted house even creepier.

The buzzing in Kimmie's head intensified, and a new vision flickered to life: Spencer, stepping onto the wooden porch and lurching forward as his foot broke through rotten wood.

"Spencer, be careful!" she cried as the vision evaporated.

But it was too late. Spencer flailed his arms, windmilling in an effort to keep his balance as the board splintered under his foot.

He dropped to his other knee with a cry of pain — followed by a lot of swear words.

"Spencer!" April ran to him as he clutched his trapped ankle, panting. "Oh my god, are you okay?"

He gritted his teeth and nodded. "I'm fine."

But Kimmie could tell he was anything but fine. His face was pale, and he was sweating profusely despite the cool night air.

Noah and Zach knelt on either side of Spencer. Noah shone his phone's light on Spencer's ankle so Zach could chip away the soft wood until Spencer could finally pull his foot free.

April whimpered when she saw the blood on his sock. "Is it bad?"

"It's nothing."

But blood welled up from a deep gash in his calf, and when April rolled his sock down, long scratches scored the skin around his ankle, and Kimmie could see at least two large splinters lodged in his flesh.

Riley dug around in her purse. "I thought I had antibiotic cream, but I can't find it."

"Don't need it," Spencer grunted as he twisted to unzip his duffel bag, then pulled out a bottle of vodka. He twisted off the cap and poured several splashes over the wounds. "Nature's antibiotic."

"That's not—"

"Jeez, Toby, read the room." Zach stood and offered Spencer a hand up.

Spencer took it. Then he put his full weight on his injured ankle.

"See? I'm fine," he told April with a forced smile. "Not going to let anything ruin tonight."

Then he yanked on the doorknob. It opened with a horror-movie creak.

"Cursed," Riley whispered to Zach.

"Rust," Zach whispered back. "Let's go get us some haunted house sex."

SIX

Kimmie set her backpack down on the dusty floor beside the plastic-covered couch in Sheila Bain's abandoned parlor. Cobwebs were everywhere, but the moonlight making it through the dusty windows outlined them with a silver glow. After Sheila died, someone must have draped all the furniture with plastic covers.

Brittany and Noah started removing them.

"It's been more than thirty years." Riley pulled a flashlight out of her tote, then dropped the bag next to Kimmie's backpack. "Why isn't it in worse shape?"

"You'd think someone would be squatting here," Spencer said.

"We don't know that there isn't until we check out the rest of the house," Noah reminded him.

"Squatters leave trash." Spencer ripped the plastic cover off a small sideboard and dumped the contents of the plastic bags — an assortment of chips, cookies, candy, and protein bars — onto it. "You could dust this place, and it'd be ready to move in."

Quinn joined him, setting her cooler next to the pile of snacks and opening it to reveal beer, wine coolers, and soda on ice. "Who's coming with me to check the upstairs?"

"It gives me the creeps," Riley said.

"No kidding." Zach set a battery-operated camping lantern on the coffee table. "It's like a set for a horror movie."

Quinn grinned. "Isn't that the point?"

"Look at this," Jenny said, pointing at a window sill in the living room.

Kimmie came closer and saw that the sill was lumpy — because someone had glued a ton of polished rocks of all shapes and sizes to the wood. She touched one with her fingertip, expecting it to be smooth, but something had been carved into the stone. An odd burning sensation crawled up her arm. She yanked her finger away, then used her phone as a flashlight to illuminate the rock she'd touched highlighting a swirly symbol, much like the ones on Jenny's pendant.

Every single stone had the same symbol inscribed on it.

The buzzing in her head surged.

"Hey, it's the same over here," Riley said. "Quartz, hematite, amethyst, agate, rose quartz."

She touched each crystal as she named it. But she didn't seem to be bothered at all.

"Is something carved in them?" Kimmie asked.

Riley looked closer. "Yeah, but I don't recognize it."

Kimmie turned to Jenny. "It's like your necklace. Can you read it?"

"It's not the same." But Jenny touched the pendant on its leather cord as if she was double-checking. "Psychics use crystals to amplify their powers all the time. Or to ground them."

"I need to set up for readings." April held up her Tarot deck. "Spence, grab us a room for later?"

"Look what I found." Toby waved an old-fashioned folding straight razor like it was a magic wand. Light glinted off the new-looking blade.

"Where did you get that?" Brittany asked, taking a couple of steps backward.

"The bathroom down the hall." Toby looked fascinated as he turned it over in the light of the camping lantern Zach had just set on the coffee table. He ran his finger along the edge, testing its sharpness, and a small trickle of blood welled up from the cut.

"Toby!" Riley scolded. "Be careful with that."

April held her hand. "Give it to me."

"I'm not going to hurt anyone," Toby said. "I just want to look at it."

"She told you to hand it over, freak."

Kimmie thought Spencer might try to wrestle the razor away from Toby. But then Noah added, "That's a serious weapon, buddy. We don't want any accidents."

Toby glared at Noah and Spencer for a moment. Then he snapped the razor shut and put it into his pocket. "Finders keepers."

"I'm not going to be shaving tonight; I'm going to be too busy doing something else." Zach pulled a fistful of condoms out of his backpack and laid them on the sideboard next to the pile of snacks. "Take as many as you need; no judgment."

Kimmie flushed and turned away, examining the fireplace. The mortar between the rough bricks was crumbling in places, and the metal screen in front was rusted in others. A small cast-iron stand held a poker, a shovel, and a small hatchet.

She squinted and bent forward to look closer at the ashes piled around the metal grate. She smelled the tang of woodsmoke and soot.

Could those ashes be thirty years old? Or had someone been using the fireplace recently?

A buzzy feeling started up again in the back of her head like a bee had somehow gotten into her brain and was trying to get out by banging into the back of her skull, over and over again. Then she noticed something else. A door at the other end of the living room, half hidden by a faded tapestry. She got to her feet and walked over to it, tugging the fabric aside to reveal the rest of the door. It was made of heavy oak, with a wrought iron handle in the shape of a coiled snake.

"What's that?" Zach asked, coming up behind her.

"I don't know." Kimmie reached out and touched the handle, half expecting it to be cold. But it was warm to the touch as if someone had been holding it moments before.

"It looks like a dungeon door," Riley said with a laugh. "Should we go explore it?"

Kimmie hesitated, then took a deep breath and turned the handle.

The door swung open with a creak, revealing a small room beyond. It was dark, but she could make out a desk covered in plastic and walls lined with shelves filled with all kinds of occult items: old books with cracked leather bindings, candles in glass jars with paintings of saints on them, creepy-looking figurines, and crystals of every color. She could see a window, covered in heavy curtains.

Kimmie pulled them aside, letting in a shaft of filtered moonlight.

"It's a witch's den," Riley said.

"Psychic's den," Zach corrected. "This must be where Sheila made her predictions."

Kimmie lifted the plastic on the desk to peek underneath. A crystal ball, an intricately-carved wooden box, and a skull. It looked real.

"Hey, that's cool!" Riley snatched the box and snapped it open. A small silk bag nestled inside.

"What is it?" Kimmie asked.

"A Tarot deck." Riley turned the bag upside down and dumped the cards onto the desk. They were old and well-worn, with faded images on the front that seemed more … primitive than the ones in April's deck.

The buzzing in Kimmie's head intensified.

She picked one up and looked at it—the Devil. Satan leered at her, tongue lolling as he held one clawed hand up in what might have been a blessing, while with the other he yanked on chains attached to the collars of a naked man and women crouched in misery before his throne.

Sheila's deck. She might have used it to learn that April's grandfather was cheating on her with April's grandmother.

Kimmie shivered as the buzzing got louder. She closed her eyes, swaying as she imagined Sheila — a fiery redhead in a flowing white gown and gold pendant inscribed with symbols Kimmie had never seen before — sitting behind the desk by candlelight, poring over the cards arranged in a cross-and-staff configuration.

A tap on her shoulder. Kimmie whirled around, raising the card in front of her face as if it would protect her from an attacker.

But it was only Noah holding out a sparkling wine cooler. Strawberry daiquiri, her favorite.

"Thanks." She took a sip, then let him lead her back into the living room, toward the couch.

Zach followed, then Riley last, after she'd gathered Sheila's cards into a pile, which she fanned out to show the group.

"Cool!" Brittany

"Those aren't nearly as pretty as mine," April sniffed.

"I found them, so I guess they're mine now." Riley put the cards back in the bag and held it out to Kimmie. "But I feel like you should hang onto them."

Kimmie took them reluctantly, and as soon as she did, the buzzing in her head quieted.

"What if they're cursed?" Brittany asked.

"If the person who cursed them is dead, then the curse is probably broken." April laid a big purple silk scarf over the coffee table and set her deck in the middle of it. "Who wants to go first?"

"Tarot cards are lame." Jenny held up a Ouija board in one hand and a planchette in the other. "Who wants to talk to a ghost?"

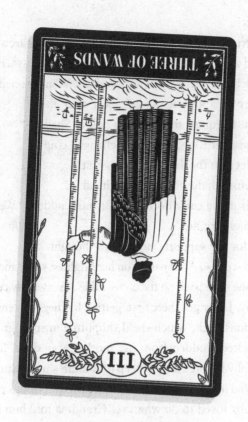

SEVEN

April stared in disbelief as everyone clustered around Jenny and her stupid Ouija board on the other end of the coffee table. Who did she think she was, telling everyone what to do when April had been planning this for months? Being Toby's date did not make Jenny part of the group.

"Everyone knows Ouija is fake," April said. "It's either gibberish, or someone is spelling out the words on purpose."

"Not when the board is being used by a true psychic."

That bitch.

"I am a true psychic; ask anyone here. My readings are always right."
April looked at Kimmie to back her up, but Kimmie just scrunched back
into the couch like she wanted to disappear. What the hell?

Was she mad about her and Spencer after all?

"It might be fun to see if we can talk to Sheila—"

April glared at Riley, and Riley changed course.

"—but let's do the Tarot readings first."

"I'm up for whatever," Quinn chimed in.

"No reason we can't do both," Brittany added. "We're going to
be here all night, right?"

Thanks for the support, guys, April thought.

But she'd won, so April pasted on her brightest smile and shuffled the
deck. Then she set it back on the coffee table. "Somebody cut the deck."

Naturally, Jenny got there first, getting her negative energy all over
April's precious deck, which she'd shoplifted in sixth grade and had
managed to keep hidden from her mother ever since. She'd had to
blackmail Toby to force him to keep his mouth shut because Grandma
Patricia was so jealous of Sheila she'd declared all things psychic to be
evil. And Toby loved to do whatever Grandma told him to.

Sicko.

April picked up the two piles of cards that Jenny had set down in the
opposite order. Then she closed her eyes and took a slow, deep breath.

Just like always, the room settled into silence.

When she opened her eyes, everyone was watching her.

"How about I draw one card for each of us to see what our night
will be like?"

No one objected, so she began.

"Kimmie." She flipped the top card over. Ace of Cups, but reversed.
April quickly turned it upright. "Oo, the beginning of a new love!"

Instead of looking happy, Kimmie looked stricken. What was wrong
with her tonight?

Jenny butted in once again. "You're not supposed to turn it over when it comes up reversed."

"Because I realize you turned the deck around when you cut it. You're not supposed to do that."

"What does it mean reversed?" Kimmie asked.

Didn't Kimmie realize that April was trying to give her a great fortune? "Barrenness, stagnation, and despair."

April wanted to slap that superior look off Jenny's face. "You know a lot about Tarot for someone who thinks it's lame."

"I messed around with them when I was younger before I realized they were a crutch." Then Jenny said to Kimmie, "Ace of Cups reversed can also mean a failure of intuition. Or that you're going to lose someone you love."

Kimmie looked like she was going to faint.

"C'mon, people, who do you want to read your cards? Me, who you've known for years? Or my brother's girlfriend, who you just met?"

"You," Brittany said too quickly. "Do mine next."

April smiled gratefully at Brittany. "How about I read for Noah first, just in case Kimmie's worried?"

April turned the deck around in her hands, then revealed the next card. "Five of Wands. Upright."

But it would've been reversed if she'd dealt it the way Jenny had handed it to her.

"Five of Wands is a card of struggle and conflict; It's true." April shot Noah what she hoped was a reassuring look. "But it also represents something of great value that can be won through ingenuity. It just means you have a test to pass."

She nodded at Kimmie. "But I know for a fact that the person giving the test wants you to get an A+."

Laughter and knowing looks all around, except for Kimmie, who was beet red and practically hyperventilating. Noah would be working hard to get Kimmie relaxed enough for what came next.

That buoyed April's spirits — the cards were right; Jenny had put them down on the coffee table the wrong way. Probably just to mess her up.

But the niggling voice in the back of her head said: it should've been reversed.

And Five of Wands, when reversed, could also symbolize avoiding a conflict instead of resolving it. Could there be something that Kimmie and Noah were going to fight about?

April cleared her throat and flipped the next card.

✦

Kimmie shook her head, trying to make the buzzy feeling go away, but instead, it got louder, bleeding from her head into the rest of her body as April flipped over each card and made her predictions.

And with each flip, a new vision flashed before Kimmie's eyes.

First, she herself in a mental hospital, dressed in a shapeless T-shirt and sweatpants, looking into April's eyes. April, sitting across from her, dressed the same, her red-gold curls were chopped short and uneven, as if she'd tried to cut her hair without a mirror. April began laying Tarot cards on the table between — Sheila's cards — in a cross-and-staff layout.

Next, Noah lying on the stained wood floor, blood pulsing out of the gaping slit beneath his chin, the puddle moving toward her as she watched, frozen.

"Brittany, Three of Cups. This one represents an abundance of love. Fertility too." April paused dramatically: "It might also predict an upcoming marriage."

Riley raised her hand like she wanted to be called on in class. "Dibs on maid of honor."

Brittany batted her eyelashes at Quinn, who glanced away.

Kimmie heard it all from a distance, her vision shifting from Noah to Brittany—

—sprawled lifelessly on a blue-and-yellow sleeping bag, a touch of something red at the corner of her mouth.

"Quinn, Page of Swords. Someone who always knows the right thing to say and how to say it in the best possible way."

"Mistress of talking dirty," Zach said.

"Or sweet-talking, you ought to try it sometime," Riley countered, which prompted Zach to grab the chain attached to her collar and pull her in for a kiss.

Quinn on the floor, her face contorted in terror, her crisp white shirt and the front of her pants soaked in blood.

"Zach, the Fool. He's enthusiastic and open to new experiences."

Zach added, "In other words, I've got ADHD, even between the sheets."

Zach hunched over, clutching his bloody stomach, then looked up and met her eyes with an anguished grimace.

"Riley, you've got … King of Pentacles?" April thought for a moment. "This one can mean someone loyal and patient—"

"Extremely patient." Riley shot Zach a pointed look.

He grinned. "That's why I love you, baby."

April cleared her throat. "It can also mean someone slow to show affection."

Riley, in shock, blood bubbling out of her mouth as she tried to say something Kimmie couldn't hear.

"The Chariot for Spencer. Someone who's used their mind to conquer their emotions — and who will be highly successful."

"Highly successful at jerking it," Zach muttered.

Spencer falling forward into Kimmie's arms, his face slashed in half a dozen places, blood spurting from his forearms, his hands hanging limp.

April turned over another card. Then silence.

"Death." That was Jenny, sounding hatefully smug.

"Which doesn't mean literal death," April said quickly. "The Death card represents transformation. Like a caterpillar turning into a butterfly."

"Destruction, too. But yeah, maybe you're a caterpillar."

April, holding a knife high overhead, snarling with fury. And somehow, the most beautiful thing Kimmie had ever seen.

April slapped another card on the table so hard that Jenny's Ouija board jumped, the planchette clattering to the floor.

"Toby, the Wheel. Reversed."

"I thought everyone gets an upright card tonight," Jenny sneered.

"My intuition is telling me this one should be reversed." April paused as if waiting for Jenny to challenge her again. But when she didn't, April continued, "Whatever tonight holds for you, it's fated. The end of a cycle, the beginning of something new."

"His date actually showed; that's something new," Spencer said.

Toby cowering on the floor, staring at something in terror, his hands raised beseechingly.

"Jenny—"

Jenny glared at April, arms crossed, one eyebrow raised.

"The High Priestess?"

"Don't you forget it," Jenny said.

Jenny, struggling to stand in waist-deep water, leaning forward as if fighting a strong current, one lace-gloved hand reaching to someone Kimmie couldn't see in the darkness.

"Who wants a snack?" Brittany jumped up and headed for the sideboard, grabbing a bag of potato chips and tossing it to Quinn, who caught it easily. Then she picked up a candy bar. "Snickers, anyone?"

"We're not done." Jenny leaned forward and turned over another Tarot card. "For Sheila. The Devil."

The same card that Kimmie had chosen from Sheila's deck. How could that be a coincidence? April's deck was more modern, the images in vibrant colors that seemed cartoonish compared to the dusty colors in Sheila's older deck. April's devil wasn't scary at all; he was mike ... like a hot, ripped guy who happened to have wings and horns.

April snatched the cards up and cut them back into her deck.

"What does the Devil mean?" Kimmie asked.

"Nothing," April answered. "Because Sheila's dead. She has no future to read."

"It signifies base energy transmuted into higher power," said Jenny.

April shoved her deck back in its bag and got up to stuff the bag into her purse, shoulder-checking Jenny as she passed.

Jenny smirked. Kimmie wished April — or anyone — would tell her to leave. Or that Toby would take her upstairs so they didn't have to listen to her creepy-ass bullshit.

"The Devil can also signify bondage to the material world or being distracted from spiritual pursuits by physical pleasures," Jenny added.

"For example, are you just here to party, or are you going to help me summon a ghost?"

"Are you some kind of witch?" Zach asked.

"My aunt's a witch," Brittany said. "I went to a Samhain ritual with her once. We all wore cloaks and sang songs about the goddess. It's all nature worship."

Kimmie didn't think Jenny was that kind of witch.

"The only other kind of witch is the kind that worships Satan."

Everyone went quiet except Jenny, who laughed at April's accusation. "Some people think that because some people are ignorant."

"And some people are fakers, pretending to be witches for attention," April said. "I guess we'll find out which one you are."

Jenny smiled, the kind of smile that isn't a smile at all.

"I guess we will."

✦

Noah stuffed a condom in his pocket from the pile Zach had dumped onto the sideboard, then turned toward Spencer and asked, in a low voice, "Are you going to stop this?"

"No, she's fun when she's angry." Spencer plucked two condoms for himself. "When we go upstairs, all that frustration turns into enthusiasm. If you hear April screaming, it'll be the good kind of screaming."

Noah contemplated Kimmie, sitting on the loveseat, staring at the Tarot deck she'd found in the dead woman's office. He'd been working up the nerve to ask her out when Spencer had transferred in from another school and chosen her. He couldn't blame Spencer, but he didn't hesitate to ask Kimmie to prom the second Spencer dumped her. He had suggested to Spencer that it wasn't cool to dump someone and immediately start dating their best friend, but Kimmie seemed cool with it.

Much cooler than he would have been in her situation.

Maybe because they'd been friends for so long while so many of April's boyfriends had come and gone. She seemed content to follow April around, existing on the periphery of April's drama. She probably knew down to the minute how long it would be before April got bored with Spencer.

Noah suspected Spencer would get bored with April as soon as she went all the way with him. Spencer was a good guy, but there was something desperate about the way he talked about April — and girls in general — in the locker room. Almost obsessive. Maybe damage from an old girlfriend, who'd made him feel insecure about himself?

Noah had been hoping that April would fill that hole in Spencer that he couldn't seem to fill by himself. But since he'd been dating her, Spencer's insecurity seemed to have gotten worse rather than better.

Maybe tonight would change that.

Noah looked at Kimmie and waved at her. She smiled and waved back.

Maybe something would change for him tonight, too.

"Thirsty?" Spencer asked, holding up a beer.

"Soda." Noah didn't want to be even a little bit wasted and risk blowing it with Kimmie.

"Pussy." Spencer threw a piece of ice at his face. "Get your own soda."

Riley threw a ratty pillow at Spencer.

"Shhh, we're starting!

EIGHT

Kimmie scooted over to make room for April on the loveseat while the others pulled chairs closer or settled on the floor around the coffee table. Except for Noah and Spencer, who were having a hushed conversation while rummaging through the cooler for drinks

Lightning cracked in the distance, and rain began to pelt the windows harder than Kimmie expected. Maybe the wind had picked up?

Jenny retrieved the planchette from the floor and moved her Ouija board to the center, so she could lean back against the couch while using it. Then she got out a permanent marker and said, "Before we contact the spirit, I need to protect all of you."

She turned to Brittany. "Give me your hand."

Brittany did, and Jenny drew what looked like a weird squiggle on the back of it. Then she drew a triangle around the squiggle.

"What does that do?" Brittany asked.

"Nothing," April said.

"It protects you from evil influences," Jenny said. "Everyone gets a sigil. . Otherwise it's not safe."

Quinn and Spencer took some convincing — Quinn worried that her church-going Mom would have a cow if she saw it, and Spencer objected to being a canvas for what he called bad art. Kimmie thought Spencer might be objecting in support of April. But when Noah pointed out they were wasting time arguing when they could've been doing other things, Spencer let Jenny draw the symbol on him.

"What about you?" Brittany asked. "You don't have a sigil."

"I don't need one; I've got this." Jenny touched her pendant.

"I can't believe everyone's into this bullshit," April muttered.

Kimmie hoped it was bullshit. She whispered to April, "It makes sense they'd want to try, considering we're spending the night in a haunted house."

Jenny pulled a large black candle out of her backpack, set it next to the board, and lit it. Then she pointed to the camping lantern. "Turn that off."

Brittany did, and the room plunged into near-darkness. The candle cast a circle of light that illuminated the board and the faces of the people closest to it — Jenny, Brittany, Riley, and Noah. Everyone else was a shadow, no matter how hard Kimmie squinted. Two of those shadows sat in chairs nearby. Spencer and Noah.

Jenny touched the pendant around her neck, then placed her fingers on the planchette. "Brittany and Kimmie, you'll help me channel Sheila's ghost."

Brittany reached for the planchette, but Kimmie stayed where she was. Jenny had already humiliated April once tonight. If she was going to do it a second time, Kimmie wouldn't be part of it.

"I'll do it," April said. "I'll know if you're making it up."

"You have to be willing to be a conduit. If you resist the process, it won't work."

"Convenient. You're already blaming me for it not working."

April crouched near Riley, who moved aside to make room for her.

"You have to relax and open up to the energies present." Jenny's voice was suddenly calm and commanding. "Slow your breathing … and relax your gaze. Let the flickering of the candle lead your mind to a deeper state."

Brittany obeyed, but April glared at Jenny, her nostrils flaring.

Jenny closed her eyes and sat up straighter. "Sheila Bain, we call to you through the veil that separates our world from the afterlife. Speak to us."

The candle sputtered, then flared brighter. The buzzing in Kimmie's head returned, and the room seemed impossibly dark outside that small circle of light.

"Speak to us," Jenny repeated.

The hair on Kimmie's arms stood up as a chill spread through her. Stop, she wanted to say, but she couldn't get enough air to speak.

"Speak to us. I command you."

The planchette began to move, slow and jerky. K.

"You're moving it," April said. "She's moving it."

I.

"Omigod," breathed Riley. "Kill? Is she going to tell us who killed her?"

M-M-I-

April yanked her hands away as the planchette drifted toward E. It stopped moving.

"See? I told you, she's making it move. She's the one who wanted Kimmie."

Jenny opened her eyes and smirked. "I theorized that Sheila wouldn't want to talk through the granddaughter of the woman who stole her husband. And it looks like I was right."

"Whatever." April stood and stomped toward Spencer and sat in the chair next to his. "I can't believe you're all falling for this."

Jenny turned toward Kimmie.

"I don't want to," Kimmie said.

"Just do it," April snapped. "Apparently, everyone else wants you to."

Did April mean it? Or would she be mad later if Kimmie caved? Do it.

The faint buzzing in Kimmie's head had somehow become a voice that sounded like a hive of bees. She shivered, rubbing her forearm as she tried to banish the goosebumps that inner voice had evoked.

Do it.

"Please, Kimmie?" Brittany asked. "Don't you want to know how Sheila died?"

Riley nodded. "If that's really her, we might be able to help her move on."

"Wouldn't that be more of an exorcism?" Zach asked.

"Sheila chose you for a reason." Kimmie had forgotten Toby was with them. He'd been so quiet since they'd made him put away the razor he'd found.

Do it; the voice buzzed louder.

Fine. After settling herself in the spot April had vacated, Kimmie took a deep breath and reached for the planchette. As soon as her fingers touched it, she felt a jolt of energy, and the buzzing quieted.

"Sheila," Jenny said, "are you still with us?"

The planchette moved slowly at first, then sped up, moving smoothly and quickly across the board to YES.

"Jenny was right," Brittany whispered.

Kimmie was glad she couldn't see April's face because she had to be furious. April was the one who'd spent years reading books about developing psychic powers — books Kimmie had kept for her because her grandmother disapproved of anything associated with Sheila Bain. They would do the meditative exercises together until Kimmie started having visions ... and April didn't.

Jenny tipped her head back dramatically like she was expecting Sheila to drop out of the ceiling.

"What do you want, spirit?"

The planchette seemed to vibrate under Kimmie's fingers as it began to move again, sending tingles up her arms. She glanced at Jenny, who seemed to be entranced, her eyes half-closed, her face half hidden by her long jet-black hair, her glittery black lips slightly parted.

Kimmie couldn't tell if she was guiding the planchette or not.

S-E-V-E-N.

"Seven, what?" Brittany asked.

The planchette flew across the board, spelling out:

S-A-C-R-I-F-I-C-E-S.

Brittany yanked her hands away, causing the planchette to flip over. Jenny woke up from her trance to glare at her. "We're not done."

"I don't want to do this anymore," Brittany said.

Kimmie didn't either. But the buzz in the back of her head had started back up when Brittany let go of the planchette. It wanted to keep going.

"See? She's faking it," April said. "She's making it all up to scare us."

"I had no idea you were going to scare so easily. We don't even know what seven sacrifices mean." She licked her lips. "Maybe the sacrifice is everyone's virginity."

"Why would Sheila give a crap about that?" Spencer asked.

"The point of the Ouija board is that we can ask her." Jenny glared at Brittany again. "Unless everyone is too scared?"

"I'm not scared," Zach said, moving closer.

Brittany let him have her seat by the coffee table, retreating to perch on the arm of Quinn's overstuffed chair.

"Five more minutes," Spencer said, "then April and I are going upstairs."

Click. Click. Click.

"Will you stop with that shit?" Spencer snapped.

Somewhere in the darkened room, Toby stopped playing with his Rubik's cube.

Jenny righted the planchette and put it in the center of the board. Then rested her fingers on it again and nodded for Zach and Kimmie to do the same.

The buzzing stopped the second Kimmie's fingers touched the plastic.

"What kind of sacrifices?" Jenny asked.

The planchette didn't move.

"What do you want?"

R-E-V-E-N-G-E.

"Revenge for what?"

M-U-R-D-E-R P-A-T-R-I-C-I-A

"This is sick!" April jumped out of her chair and grabbed the Ouija board.

"Give it back!" Jenny lunged for the board, but April yanked it out of reach and slammed over the back of a chair, breaking it in half.

"How dare you use this dumb game to threaten to kill my grandmother!"

April threw the board on the floor, then whirled around, landing a slap on Jenny's cheek.

"Don't hit her!" Toby emerged into the circle of light, pulling Jenny back so April couldn't reach her, while Quinn and Riley grabbed April's arms.

"Let go of me!"

The buzzing in Kimmie's head became a roar, and halos of white light engulfed everything. She scrambled backward blindly, trying to get clear of the scuffle before someone stepped on her, but she ran into something hard.

She looked up into the eyes of a corpse-pale woman in a flowing white dress that fluttered around her like it was alive—bruises around her neck. Water dripped from her hair. The antique Tarot deck in one hand and a single card face-out in the other: The Tower.

Kimmie screamed.

ACE OF CUPS

NINE

"What did she look like?"

"Did she say anything?"

"Is she still here?"

But the question that mattered most was the one that hurt: "Why are you taking her side?"

"I'm not," Kimmie said to April. "I really did see her."

"Right, another one of your 'visions.'"

Behind April, Spencer smirked, and Kimmie realized he was enjoying the show of their argument. I wasn't wrong; he did go after April to hurt me.

And he would use this to pry them further apart if he could.

But she couldn't say that to April because April would accuse her of being jealous. Either way, Kimmie lost.

"You agreed that those visions weren't real," April pushed. "That's why you gave up on our psychic exercises."

She couldn't argue with that, not without admitting she'd been lying to her best friend for years. Worse, she'd been humoring April's belief that she had psychic abilities because she needed to believe it. Kimmie had never understood why. Psychics saw things that weren't there. What was the difference between a vision and a hallucination?

"You were freaking out, just like the rest of us, and you imagined it. C'mon, admit it, Kimmie."

"Sheila decided to show herself to you. That means something." Jenny was the only person keeping her cool. Did that mean April was right about her faking the whole thing?

No, making the Ouija board talk was one thing. How could she make Kimmie see a ghost? Even if she had one of those hologram projectors, wouldn't everyone else see it too?

"She was holding a card," Kimmie said. "The Tower."

"That fits," Jenny said. But she didn't explain why.

"Kimmie imagined Sheila holding the Tower because it's the closest thing in the deck to a house." April turned to Kimmie, and spoke to her like she was a frightened puppy who didn't understand how the scary-loud vacuum cleaner worked. "This house is creepy. Jenny's pretending it's haunted—"

"It is haunted."

"—and your subconscious flashed on the things that are freaking you out. It's not a vision, Kimmie; It's just your imagination."

Everyone was watching, waiting to see if she was going to say the terrifying thing or the reassuring thing.

But Kimmie was really choosing between Jenny and April.

No contest.

"It probably was my imagination. I did drink my wine cooler kind of fast."

April rewarded Kimmie with a smile, then ruined it with a vindictive glare at Jenny.

"Enough haunted house, it's happy fun time," Spencer announced.

As everyone grabbed their bags and headed upstairs, Kimmie retrieved Sheila's Tarot deck from the loveseat where she had left it and fanned the cards until she found the Tower. But it didn't start the buzz back up, and Sheila's ghost did not appear before her.

"Was it upright or reversed?"

Kimmie jumped as Jenny seemed to suddenly be there.

"Upright." She felt like a traitor for asking, but— "What do you think it means?"

"I think it means you should enjoy your date because tonight, we're in the hands of destiny."

"I'm sorry I asked."

Jenny smiled sadly, and for the first time, she seemed like a real person instead of a goth doll brought to life. Someone Kimmie might actually like, if she got to know her.

"I feel like that all the time."

"Then why do you do this?" Kimmie asked. "Why not just be normal?"

"Sometimes life doesn't give you a choice."

✦

It's mating season, thought Toby. His lip curled. He could imagine the mating dances going on upstairs. It was ridiculous at best, a bunch of people being puppeted by their hormones, their reproductive drives telling them what to do with their lives. It had nothing to do with love. It wasn't even practical. Spencer had nothing in common with April. There was no mental connection.

And Noah had nothing in common with Kimmie. She was a spiritual person, not religious truly spiritual. She was like an angel, and Noah an earthly turd.

Maybe Riley and Zach had more connecting them, but mostly they seemed to get off on being misfits. That was just pathetic, two losers trying to lose a little less.

And then there were Quinn and Brittany. He had to admit they had a lot in common. Like sisters. Which was problematic in its own way when you thought about it.

Jenny cleared her throat. "If you ever tell anyone I said this, I will kill you. But prom was fun."

Toby laughed. "For a meaningless ritual being performed mindlessly by hundreds of morons, it was just swell."

Jenny smiled. Toby liked her a lot better when she wasn't playing Goth Barbie.

But then she had to go and ruin it. "You looked like you were having quite a conversation with Kimmie on the dance floor. What was that about?"

Toby felt himself flushing. He didn't need Sabrina the Teenage Witch sticking her nose into his business, not at this fragile stage. The seed has been planted, and he would nurture it until Kimmie was his.

It didn't matter that Kimmie was upstairs, letting Noah sweat all over her.

The thought made him gag.

"Is something wrong?" said Jenny. "You look angry. Was it something I said?"

Toby laughed. "What could you ever say that would make me mad?"

Jenny narrowed her eyes.

"Thanks ... I think." She looked around, then gestured at a small door on the wall behind them. "Now that we've got some time, I want to go through Sheila's office. See what else I can learn about her."

Toby shrugged and followed her when she stood.

It was a tiny office. Chunks of broken glass littered the floor. It smelled like dust and mildew. A few rotted scarves were draped here and there. Toby immediately disliked it.

But Jenny looked enraptured. "I can feel her energy, even after all this time. Sheila was a powerful psychic."

"This is a con artist's home office."

"You don't believe in ghosts?" Jenny asked. "Not even a little bit of doubt?"

"I'm officially keeping my mind open." Inwardly, Toby couldn't help but feel that all of this was superstitious nonsense. His grandmother had raised him to stay clear of all of it. Not because it was fake and a waste of time, but because she said it was dangerous to a person's immortal soul.

Sometimes, you have to think like a sheep to be a shepherd, thought Toby.

Kimmie believed in all kinds of crap. That meant he had to at least understand it well enough that he could break down her defenses. Otherwise, he was never going to get her to trust him.

Jenny was picking up books at random and examining them. "Maybe we can learn something useful."

"Like what?"

"Like how to control a ghost." She gestured dramatically, and spoke in a wavering, spooky voice "O ye spirits, I command you! Speak! Tell us what awaits us beyond the grave." She dropped the act, laughing at herself. "Wouldn't that be cool? Like, we could find out all the secrets of the universe now instead of waiting until we die."

"What makes you think you get any answers when you die?" scoffed Toby.

"That's what happens." Jenny was serious.

Toby dropped his gaze from her intensity. "I know you've got this idea that Kimmie is a psychic, but I want you to promise not to drag her into doing something stupid."

"Stupid?" Jenny had her nose buried in a dusty book. "Like what?"

He imagined Kimmie naked and tied down in a pentagram, getting sacrificed. "I don't know; just promise me you won't let her get hurt."

"I don't know what you see in her, but fine, I promise." She picked up another book, and thumbed through the pages. "Kimmie will be just fine."

"Thank you." He looked around. Fake or not, being in the 'psychic studio' was grating on his nerves. Or maybe it was Jenny, who had lost interest in him and was busy making a small stack of books on the table.

Toby went back to the living room, flopped on the couch, and fished his Rubik's cube out of his pocket. The smooth, familiar click-click-click was soothing.

He solved the cube and then scrambled it and started again.

TEN

April smiled in relief. The room Spencer had snagged for them was in much better shape than she'd expected. Sheila's bedroom, with all the furniture still under plastic, just like the living room. Plus, all those crazy rocks glued to the window sills.

It was kind of sad. She'd had no one to pack up her things after she died. The house had been left to rot, a monument to how much the town had disliked the dead woman.

Spencer lifted one corner of the plastic bed cover to reveal a faded bedspread in a blue-and-green floral with ruffles. Not very witchy, if you asked April.

"Should we …?" Spencer pointed to the bed.

She shuddered. "Who knows what bugs are living in that mattress?"

So Spencer unrolled the foam camping mat he'd brought while April lit her lavender-vanilla candle and set it on the window sill. She wasn't going to let Jenny ruin tonight. Or Kimmie, either. How could Kimmie even think of taking that bitch's side over April's?

Something brushed the skin between her shoulder blades. She yelped, whirling around to find Spencer, surprised and shirtless, hands raised in the air.

"I was trying to unzip your dress. I thought it would be sexy." Oh. "Go ahead."

She turned back around, suddenly thinking of Kimmie. Except Kimmie hadn't kissed the back of her neck while zipping her up. And her hands hadn't peeled the shimmery red fabric down to reveal April's—

"Wait." What was wrong with her? "Let me do it."

Spencer stepped back. She'd thought it would be more fun to strip for him, but it felt awkward and weird, like she was shedding her skin instead of her prom dress.

"Nice," Spencer said anyway. And April wondered if he'd said that to Kimmie too when he was trying to persuade her.

She pushed that thought away and kissed him, trying not to think about Jenny or Kimmie or how no one had cared about her readings, but they couldn't wait for Jenny to pull out her Ouija board and—

"Ow!" Spencer pulled back and rubbed his lip. "You bit me."

"Sorry. I still can't believe Kimmie—"

"Jesus, enough about Kimmie. Unless she's the person you'd rather be with tonight?"

For some reason, that made April even madder. "Of course not."

"Then see if you can kiss me without trying to eat my face off."

"It's just that—"

Spencer kissed her again, grabbing her hair and tugging it just hard enough to make April forget about everything but his lips and his body pressed against her and his other hand moving up and down the length of her back.

But there was one thing missing. "How come you're not—"

"Give me a minute."

✦

Kimmie trudged upstairs to the middle bedroom where Noah said he'd wait for her. Spencer and April had already claimed the big one, and Quinn and Brittany were in the smallest. Zach and Riley had taken the attic, leaving Toby and Jenny to make do with what little privacy they could manage downstairs. Kimmie wondered if they'd risk the living room or use Sheila's creepy office, with all those weird little statues staring down at them.

She shuddered at the mental image of Toby and Jenny making out on the plastic-covered desk. Gross.

As she reached for the doorknob, Kimmie heard angry murmurs. Sheila? No, Quinn and Brittany, at the end of the hall. She couldn't make out any words, but they were definitely fighting. About Sheila and Jenny? Or was it April's marriage prediction that had sparked their argument? Brittany had clearly loved the idea, but Quinn seemed uncomfortable.

The door opened, revealing Noah. He'd taken off his sport coat but was otherwise fully dressed. "Are you going to stand out in the hallway all night?"

Kimmie flushed and entered the room, which had been set up like a study — bookshelves filled with rows of books, a small writing desk, and a floor lamp beside it. Noah had removed the plastic sheet that had covered the desk and put a small candle in a jar on it to light the room. Except for the dust and the cobwebs in the corners, it was surprisingly clean. Where are all the bugs? Or the spiders that made all those webs?

What bothered Kimmie the most was the rocks glued to the window-sill. She decided not to check whether they also had the same symbol carved into them over and over again.

Sheila was a psychic. Her house was going to be weird. Carved rocks were no big deal. The Tarot deck was much creepier, and that was just a bunch of old drawings.

Noah had arranged a sleeping bag on the floor for them, which he'd unzipped and laid out like a blanket.

Kimmie flushed harder. "I ... should I take off my clothes?"

"No, just sit here with me."

So she joined him on the sleeping bag, sitting across from him. In the candlelight, Noah looked older. And even more handsome.

"Do you have the, uh—" She couldn't bring herself to say the word condom, even though they'd talked about it before. But then they were talking about the idea of sex. It wasn't theoretical anymore. It was about to become real.

"Yes." He leaned forward and kissed her, his lips soft at first and harder as she kissed him back. His hand crept up her thigh, pushing her dress up as he moved his hand higher. She gasped — no one had ever touched her there before.

"Do you want me to stop?" he whispered.

Did she? "I don't think so."

But if they kept going, he would want to take her clothes off, and even though that was the point of this whole evening, a part of her didn't want to be naked with him. It was different with April, who didn't want her. Noah did want her, which was terrifying for reasons Kimmie couldn't explain.

She grabbed the necklace that April had lent her and stared at the dancing flame of the candle, promising herself that Noah was safe, that everything would be fine, and that all she had to do was relax.

So she told him to keep doing that, and as long as he didn't try to undress her, she let him do what he wanted. Let his fingers wander further, doing things Kimmie had dreamed about doing with April. It felt good,

The buzzing came out of nowhere, filling her head with white static, and then she was in April's room. Not April's room today — it was April's room in grade school, back when they first met. Maybe before they met, because the teddy bear with the cowboy hat, April's favorite stuffie, wasn't on her desk.

Kimmie heard cards being shuffled. Where was it coming from? Under the bed.

She laid down on the floor to look, and there was eleven-year-old April, flashlight between her teeth, struggling to shuffle a Tarot deck whose cards were too big for her hands. Her elbow bumped the pile of books about Tarot interpretation beside her, knocking one out from under the bed.

"What's this?"

April froze at the sound of her grandmother's voice, followed by footsteps. A manicured hand picked the book off the floor.

"April Marie Newsome, you come out from under that bed right now."

Kimmie stayed crouched on the other side of the bed, praying that April's grandmother wouldn't see her. She watched April frantically gather the cards and shove them into a rip in the box spring seconds before the manicured hand reached under the bed and closed around April's ankle. April screamed as her grandmother dragged her out.

"Where are those devil cards?" Mrs. Newsome demanded. "I know you have them. I heard you playing with them."

"No, Grandma! I got rid of them like you said!"

Kimmie froze as Mrs. Newsome peeked under the bed from the other side. But somehow, she didn't see Kimmie, just the books, which she retrieved and threw on the bed.

"I'm taking away your library card since you can't follow my rules."

"Grandma, no!"

A loud thwack and April howled. Another thwack. And another.

It took Kimmie a moment to realize that April's grandmother was hitting her with one of the books.

Kimmie squirmed under the bed and shoved her fist against her mouth, tears burning her eyes, holding her breath and willing it to be over.

How had she not realized?

She thought about how April had begged her to keep her Tarot deck and all the library books at her place and how adamant she was that Kimmie help her practice her psychic skills. She'd never thought about how they'd never done anything with the cards when Kimmie was staying over with April.

A pair of sneakers appeared in the doorway of April's room and stopped. Toby, she guessed. Watching while April wailed.

Grandma Patricia said, "Your sister's been bad, Tobias. But you're my good boy, aren't you?"

Kimmie wanted to be sick.

The blows stopped, and April's howling became a whimper.

"You think about what you've done, and then we'll talk about privileges."

Once she was sure Mrs. Newsome had left, Kimmie crawled out from under the bed and stood. "April."

April didn't seem to hear her. She stayed curled up in a ball, crying quietly.

"April, why didn't you tell me?"

"She was ashamed," a woman's voice said from the doorway.

But it wasn't Mrs. Newsome.

It was Sheila.

❖

"Kimmie, what's wrong?" Kimmie opened her eyes. Noah hovered over her, wearing nothing but his underwear, which— oh my god.

She blushed and forced her eyes back up to his face.

"I have to check on April." She sat up. And realized she was nearly naked too.

This was ten times more embarrassing than when April saw her in her underwear. She reached for her dress, but Noah stopped her with a gentle hand on her shoulder.

"Hey, don't freak out; we can slow down. We don't have to do anything you don't want to."

He was so nice, he didn't deserve to be her rebound. Or whatever this was.

"Sheila's after April," Kimmie said. "I need to make sure she's okay."

"Spencer is not going to appreciate that."

"I don't care if Spencer hates me." He probably does already.

"But April will care, and if you keep trying to interfere—"

"As long as she's alive to hate me." Kimmie squirmed out of reach and snatched her dress off the floor, throwing it on over her head. "I'll be right back."

She didn't wait for a response, just hurried out into the hall and opened the door to the room where April and Spencer were—

—ignoring each other.

"It's not a big deal—" Spencer started.

"I don't understand what I'm doing wrong." April looked like she was close to tears. "Is it because I'm not Kimmie?"

"No, I—" Spencer noticed Kimmie in the doorway and jumped to his feet. "What the fuck?"

"I— I just needed to see—"

"See what?" April demanded. "Are you so hung up on Spencer that you need to spy on us while we're having sex?"

"She was worried." Noah, who'd put his slacks back on before coming to back her up. "She thought she saw the ghost."

Then he frowned and looked at Kimmie. "Or did you hear the ghost?"

"I had a vision," Kimmie blurted. "Of your Grandma hitting you with a book. Sheila was there, and I thought it meant she was coming for you."

April stared at Kimmie for so long that Kimmie wondered if she'd heard.

Then she said, "You. Are. Unbelievable."

And slammed the door in Kimmie's face.

❖

April turned back around — and stopped when she saw the bulge in Spencer's boxers. Fury swirled through her, even more intense than before.

"So, fully-dressed Kimmie is more interesting than me almost naked?"

"No, I—"

"Then what? Is Noah the reason for your boner?"

"Fuck you." Spencer grabbed his pants and started yanking them on. "I thought you'd be a lot more fun, but you can't be away from Kimmie for more than two seconds."

Her body moved before she had time to think — she slapped him so hard that the shock of the blow resonated up her arm. Pain flared in the palm of her hand, and her fingers went numb as his head whipped sideways.

When he turned back to her, the rage in his eyes matched her own. He shoved her, and she fell backward, landing flat on her back, and a second later, he was on top of her.

He kissed her viciously, pinning her so she couldn't move. Couldn't breathe.

At least he was paying attention to her now.

THE FOOL

ELEVEN

The storm had gotten worse. Much worse. Rain pounded on the roof like it was trying to punch through the shingles. But Riley didn't hear the sound of dripping water, and the floor looked dry. No leaks in a house this old?

"Whoa, look at this!" Zach exclaimed.

Riley came closer as he raised his camping lantern higher, revealing an elaborate pentagram painted on the attic floor in red paint, with smaller symbols painted around the outside of the circle and in the five points of the star within.

Zach beamed at her. He couldn't have been more pleased if he'd painted the pentagram just for her instead of discovering it.

"Is this the best haunted house you'll ever have sex in, or what?"

Riley smiled back, set her bag down, and then hugged him. "You've been promising me haunted house sex for ages. Time to put out."

He rewarded her with a slow kiss, then pulled away and laid down in the center of the star, spread-eagled.

"Now that you've summoned me from hell, Mistress ..." He rolled over onto his side, pouting seductively. "Will there be chanting, or can we skip straight to the part where we sacrifice the virgin?"

"I think we're ready to sacrifice the virgin."

Riley pushed him back and straddled him, barely holding back her laughter. Neither of them qualified as virgins and hadn't since the beginning of senior year — not that it was anyone's business. When everyone had started planning for prom, Riley and Zach had agreed to go along with it and act like it was their first time. She loved the idea that it was their secret, just like she loved how Zach had agreed to elope with her after graduation. It would be the two of them against the world like it had been since freshman year.

"First, I think I'll—"

Nausea rolled through Riley, and she pitched forward, one hand hitting the floor as she slapped the other over her mouth. It's too soon for morning sickness.

Another secret, but this one she hadn't told Zach. Not until she was sure.

"Babe?" she heard him say, as if from very far away.

She closed her eyes and breathed slowly, trying to catch her breath.

"Babe!"

The dizziness faded. But when she opened her eyes, something was still wrong.

Zach was lying on carpet.

They weren't in the attic anymore.

"How did we—"

"I don't know," Zach answered. "One second, we were there, then I blinked, and we were here."

Here was a dimly-lit room that looked like it had been dressed for a movie set in Victorian England: huge chairs upholstered in leather, a desk, and small tables that could've been looted from an antique store. In one corner, a full suit of armor. In another corner, a huge stuffed dog reared up and bared its massive teeth. And on the walls, were all sorts of weapons — swords, spears, knives, axes — as well as what looked like torture devices. On the wall behind the desk hung a painting of a pale cliff overlooking the sea, a big orange sun in the corner.

Riley swallowed hard. "I think we should go."

"Agreed." Zach got to his feet and held out a hand to help her up. "But how?"

He looked around the room, then went to one of the walls and tugged on a sword. It didn't budge.

"Huh. That's weird."

He tried a few more weapons with the same result.

"It's like they're glued to the wall or something."

Riley went to the door and tried the handle. "It's locked."

Her rattles were no use.

"We're trapped in here," she said, her voice trembling slightly.

"Don't worry." Zach came up behind Riley and wrapped his arms around her waist. "We'll figure this out."

She wanted to believe him. "Maybe there's a secret door?"

"I'll check. Why don't you see if there's a key or something in the desk?"

Zach started knocking on walls.

Riley went to the desk and started going through the drawers. The first two were empty, but she found an old-fashioned six shooter in the third. It was heavier than she expected, but somehow it felt familiar in her hand, even though she'd never touched a gun. The metal had a dark oily finish, but the pearl grip gleamed like trapped moonlight.

"Zach, I think I found something."

He turned around as she held it up to examine it better. But nausea ripped through her again, and searing pain on the back of her hand so intense, it blurred her vision.

She fought to suck in a breath.

She heard the sound of rushing water. It flooded over her feet, so cold they instantly went numb. And then it rose to her ankles.

Where was it coming from?

EIGHT OF CUPS

TWELVE

Kimmie bolted up the stairs to the attic, heart pounding in her chest almost as loud as Noah's footsteps behind her. That impossible gunshot sounded like it was right overhead. It had to be Jenny. Kimmie couldn't imagine her friends bringing a gun to prom, not even Toby.

The hair on the back of her neck stood up as she entered the attic. Riley lay facedown on the floor, sprawled like she'd fallen from a great height. She was soaking wet from head to toe, and a puddle of water spread out around her.

And Zach …

Zach hunched over, clutching his bloody stomach, then looked up and met her eyes with an anguished grimace.

Just like in her vision.

Zach collapsed at the center of the pentagram with a groan. On the ground next to him — The Fool. From Sheila's Tarot deck.

He was soaked too.

Kimmie was suffocating, fear clogging her throat, so she couldn't breathe in or out. Couldn't move. She was made of ice, and any second now, she would shatter.

Noah rushed past Kimmie and dropped to his knees beside Zach, touching his fingers to his friend's neck. "I think he's dead."

Kimmie hurried to Riley and rolled her over. She whimpered, her eyes fluttering open. Then she saw Zach.

She screamed like her soul was being torn from her body as she crawled toward him until she was finally close enough to press her face into his chest. Then she screamed again.

Noah tried to pull her away, but she clawed at him, leaving bloody marks across his face. The second he let go of her, she threw herself on Zach's body again.

Kimmie shoved her panic down and forced herself to take a breath. And another. Until she could breathe without having to think about it.

"What the fucking hell?" Spencer had arrived, and a step behind him, April, murmuring no no no no no under her breath.

"Where's Jenny?" Kimmie asked.

"She's right here." Toby emerged from the staircase, followed by Jenny. "What happ—"

"Where was she?" Kimmie struggled to keep her voice even. "Where was she when Zach was shot?"

Jenny grabbed the banister, apparently needing the support to make it up the last couple of steps.

But Toby seemed surprised. "Downstairs, with me. She didn't do this."

"Well, none of us did it," April said. "And she's the only one who was talking about murder. And sacrifices."

"That was Sheila," Jenny said.

"You were making the board say it."

"Kimmie and Brittany had their fingers on the planchette too."

April practically shrieked, "But they wouldn't kill Zach!"

"How did Zach get shot?" Kimmie asked.

"The gun," Riley sobbed. "I found it in the desk."

Kimmie looked around the attic, which was empty except for a stack of boxes in one corner. "What desk?"

"I was looking for the key ..." Riley broke into sobs again, and this time she let Noah pull her away from Zach's body.

He rubbed her back awkwardly until she could talk again.

"I don't know how we got there. We were In a locked room with swords on the walls and leather chairs. And a big stuffed dog. Almost as big as a wolf."

"A dog?" April scoffed.

"A hallucination," Toby said. "Grandma Patricia says weed can make you have a psychotic break."

Kimmie shushed them both. "Riley, what happened?"

"I know what I saw—a dog. And ..." Riley grimaced like it hurt to remember. "... there were swords and spears and other weapons glued to the walls."

Spencer guffawed, but Noah elbowed him, and he shut up.

"I found the gun in the bottom drawer of the desk. Then I felt dizzy. And I think my hand was on fire."

Riley glanced down at her hand and started hyperventilating. "What? The? Hell?"

Noah grabbed her wrist and raised it so they all could see — the symbol of protection that Jenny had drawn on the back of Riley's hand with the marker now looked like it had been burned into the skin.

Branded.

Kimmie checked the back of her own hand, but her symbol was still written in marker.

"What does that mean?" April asked.

"It means she did this." Spencer pointed at Jenny. "I don't know how, but it's the only explanation."

"You're accusing me because you don't want to believe the obvious. That Riley shot Zach with a gun she found."

"In a room that doesn't exist!" Spencer snapped. "We've been in every room of this house. Have you seen one with a stuffed dog and a bunch of weapons lying around?"

"Why would Riley kill Zach?" April asked. "They were more in love than any of us."

She glanced at Spencer, but he didn't deny it. Kimmie wondered if April had thought that having sex with Spencer would make him fall in love with her.

"Maybe it's the serial killer," Kimmie said. "The one that killed Maisie."

"We checked out the whole house when we got here," Spencer reminded her. "Where would a serial killer hide?"

"Unless the serial killer is one of us." April glared at Jenny, who stared coolly back at her.

She dresses scary, but that doesn't mean she's a serial killer. But April was so clearly in a mood that Kimmie didn't dare say it out loud. It would probably be a long time before April forgave Jenny for doubting her psychic abilities and dissing her Tarot readings. If Jenny had actually killed Zach — April would hate her forever.

Kimmie would too. But it wasn't fair to blame her without evidence.

"She invited herself," April continued. "And—

"She didn't invite herself; I invited her." Toby stepped forward to stand beside Jenny.

April rolled her eyes. "That doesn't mean she's not a serial killer; It just means you have poor judgment."

"If anyone is a serial killer, it's probably the person whose idea it was to spend the night here," Jenny countered.

"We need to call the police." Noah stuck his hands in his pants pockets but came up empty. "It's their job to figure out what's happening."

"Oh god, I'm going to jail!" Riley wailed.

"We won't let that happen," April said, taking Riley's hand and holding it in both of hers. "We'll explain that it was an accident. Or self-defense. There's no gun with your fingerprints, so there's no evidence."

"That we've found," Jenny added.

Was Jenny trying to piss April off, or could she not help saying the most unhelpful thing possible?

Spencer pulled his phone out of his pocket. Water dribbled out of the sides. "Anybody got a bag of rice I can borrow?"

Kimmie walked around to the other side of Zach's body, trying not to look at him as she inched toward the card. It didn't disappear when she tried to pick it up.

One corner was sticky with blood. But she couldn't tell if it was from the deck she'd found or another one.

Jenny had come here prepared to summon Sheila — or to make it seem like she had. What if she knew more about the dead psychic than she'd said?

Or maybe this wasn't about magic at all. Had there been time for Jenny to sneak upstairs, hypnotize (or perhaps, drug?) Riley, kill Zach, brand Riley's hand, then sneak back downstairs?

Seemed unlikely. And even if it was possible, why? Jenny barely knew any of them.

But what other logical explanation was there?

That Jenny had somehow tricked Riley into killing Zach?

That Riley and Zach had found a secret room? And Zach's death was an accident?

That a vengeful ghost had killed Zach?

✦

Ten minutes later, everyone had given up on getting a cell signal.

"New plan," said Noah. "We all go down to our rooms and get our things. We go outside; we call the police. Until they arrive, everyone stays together, no matter what. Horror movie rules."

"What are horror movie rules?" Toby asked.

"No splitting up," April said, ticking them off on her fingers. "No checking out weird noises. And most of all, no going into the basement. Ever."

Noah and Spencer half-carried Riley between them as they trudged down to the second story, where Jenny helped Kimmie and April pack up in silence.

Toby walked further down the hall — but still visible to Noah and Spencer — and knocked on the door of Quinn and Brittany's room.

When they didn't answer, he knocked again. "Hey, open up; we're leaving."

Still no answer.

"Maybe they passed out?" he suggested.

"They might not be decent." Kimmie grabbed her bag and joined Toby. "You wait here; I'll check."

But as soon as she turned the knob, she knew something was wrong. The room was empty except for a small lantern, Quinn's duffel, and a picnic blanket on the floor.

"They must already be downstairs," she said. "Maybe they panicked when they heard the gunshot and decided to leave."

Toby shrugged. "Sounds like a good idea to me."

So they all filed to the staircase. But when they got to the bottom floor, Quinn and Brittany weren't there either.

"Would they have left without telling us?" April wondered.

"They must have," Spencer said. "We've been in every room in this house, and we haven't seen them."

"The sooner the police get here, the sooner they can find Quinn and Brittany." Noah shouldered his bag, walked to the front door, and grabbed the doorknob.

But when he tried to pull the door open, it stuck.

"The knob turns," he said after several tries. "It just won't open."

"Let me," Spencer said.

But he couldn't open it either.

"Fuck this." Spencer picked up the cooler and lobbed it at the window. It bounced off.

Snarling, he stomped to the dining room and returned with a chair, which he swung at the window, feet first.

The chair bounced off the window, too, killing his balance and making him spin around.

He took several steps back, held the chair in front of him like a battering ram, and charged at the window.

When the chair hit the window, it just …stopped. And Spencer sailed across the room, slamming into the far wall, then sliding down into a crouch.

He wheezed as Noah pulled him to his feet, struggling to catch his breath.

April started to sniffle. "How can this be happening?"

Kimmie didn't answer. She knew how this could be happening and wanted to be wrong.

She pulled the Fool card out of her bag and laid it on the coffee table. Then she retrieved Sheila's deck and started going through it, one card at a time.

No Fool.

She counted them, laying the cards in stacks of ten, until there were seven left over.

But a Tarot deck had seventy-eight cards. Which meant the card she'd found by Zach's body belonged to Sheila's deck.

But that deck had been in the room with Kimmie and Noah up until they heard the gunshot.

"Sheila wants seven sacrifices," Riley said. "I don't think she will let us leave until she's got all seven."

"Shut up and let me think," April snapped.

"I never told Zach," Riley quavered. "He's never going to know that I was— that we were going to—"

She covered her face with her hands and started crying.

Jenny walked over to the coffee table and picked up her Ouija board. "If we talk to Sheila again, maybe she'll tell us—"

"Shut up." April glared at her. "It's your fault Zach is dead."

"That's not fair," Toby said. "Jenny's not the one who shot him."

Riley's cries turned to sobs.

April turned on Toby. "It's your fault too; you invited her."

"If we just—" Jenny started.

"SHUT UP." April shoved Jenny, forcing her to take a step back. "Or I will sacrifice you."

"No one is sacrificing anyone."

Kimmie wondered how Noah could still be so calm.

"If we can't leave," he continued, "then we stay here in this room until the sun comes up and people come looking for us."

April brightened. "I told dozens of people we were spending the night here."

"See?" Noah said. "All we have to do is stay put and stay together, and we'll be safe."

Kimmie's toes turned prickly-cold. She stomped her foot to warm it up — and heard a splash.

Water on the floor, almost an inch deep.

And rising.

THREE OF CUPS

THIRTEEN

"Where is it coming from?"

"Is the roof leaking?"

"How can it be coming in so fast?"

Kimmie paused on the second-story landing of the staircase and looked down while the others argued. Water had swallowed the bottom two steps and began to creep toward the third.

Just like in her dream.

But in her dream, she'd been alone, except for Maisie. None of the others had been with her.

Unless... they were, but they were all dead? And how could Maisie have been there?

Could Maisie have been a ghost? She'd bled in the dream. Kimmie had felt the resistance of her flesh as the knife sank into it. The slick heat of Maisie's blood spurting all over her face and her hands. Her palms still remembered the rough texture of the dagger's metal handle, even though she'd never physically touched it.

Kimmie forced herself to breathe through the panic that threatened to swamp her. Her head buzzed as the room started to tilt. She reached for the wall with numb hands to keep from falling over as she blew the air out slowly and counted to eight.

Just like her therapist had taught her.

I am dreaming. Dreams can't hurt me. Dreams aren't true.

But she didn't wake up in her bedroom, even though she repeated it as she felt her way along the wall to the open doorway of the biggest bedroom.

Riley slumped on the plastic-covered bed, head down, elbows on her knees. Toby sat nearby and had his Rubik's cube out, twisting it as he watched Spencer and Noah try to open the window that looked out over the backyard. April paced, arms crossed over her stomach.

Jenny sat crossed-legged with her Ouija board on her lap. She gestured for Kimmie to join her.

Hell no.

Kimmie grabbed Sheila's deck and began sorting through it.

Oh, shit. One was a coincidence, but two?

She gathered her courage and said, "I had a dream, and I think it's coming true."

Everyone looked at her except Jenny, who seemed to be studying the board. The only sound in the room was the click-click-click of Toby's Rubik's cube.

"What are you talking about?" April asked.

So Kimmie told them about the whirlpool, drowning but not drowning, and killing Maisie. Then she explained about how the cards she'd found by the bodies were missing from her deck.

When she finished, Spencer laughed.

"This isn't a dream, in case you hadn't noticed," April said. "Also, Maisie isn't trying to kill us; Sheila is."

"Maybe it's Maisie pretending to be Sheila," Toby said. "She was the last person to die in this house."

"Or maybe it's Sheila pretending to be Maisie."

Beneath her heavy makeup, Jenny seemed even paler to Kimmie in the moonlight shining through the window.

The window that Noah and Spencer still hadn't managed to open.

"What do we know about the night Maisie died?" Kimmie asked.

April started ticking them off. "That she slit her own throat. That the other kids who were with her said she went nuts. That the sister who found her got sent away. That the sheriff couldn't find the knife."

"Her boyfriend Jacob was on the basketball team with my cousin." Noah continued to mess with the window latch. "He said Maisie attacked him with a spear. But ... my cousin also said that Jacob was pretty high that night."

Jenny hesitated, then said, "Given how Zach died, maybe we should assume he was telling the truth."

"Nobody cares what you think!" April snapped.

"The water is real; I'm still wet from it," Kimmie said. "The brand on Riley's hand is real. The gunshot wound is real, even though we haven't found the gun. Maybe we're high, and we're all sharing one big group hallucination, but "

"But we should assume it's all real," Riley said in a monotone.

"FUCK." Spencer threw himself at the window like he was blocking a tackle. He bounced backward and landed on his ass. "FUCK!"

Kimmie held up Sheila's deck. "The Fool card we found next to

Zach — I think it came from this. The Three of Cups is missing too."

"So you're the killer?" April asked. "You're the one who's been carrying that deck around all night."

"Kimmie was with me." It felt less like Noah was defending her and more like he was pointing out the obvious, but Kimmie was still grateful he'd said it.

A long pause, where everyone seemed to be staring off into space.

Click.

Click.

Click.

"Knock that off," Spencer said to Toby.

"It helps me think."

"Yeah?" Spencer jumped to his feet and grabbed the Rubik's cube. "Well, it doesn't help me think."

"Give it back!" Toby lurched to his feet and jumped for it, but Spencer wasn't just taller; he was also a quarterback used to dodging guys much bigger and faster than Toby.

Spencer ran out into the hallway and threw Toby's Rubik's cube down the stairs, where it landed with a loud splash. "If you want it, go get it."

Toby turned to the rest of them. "You saw what he did. He's bullying me."

April shrugged. "Who cares? You'll probably die before you would've solved it anyway."

Toby looked at Kimmie, but what was she supposed to do? Dive down into the water and get his toy for him?

"Does anyone have a multitool?" Noah asked. "Or even a pocket knife?"

"Maybe we should try talking to Sheila," Kimmie suggested. "Negotiate with her."

"Why do you keep taking her side?" April pointed an accusing finger at Jenny. "We wouldn't be in this mess if you hadn't agreed to do the stupid board with her in the first place."

"You're the one who wanted to spend the night in this stupid house."

Kimmie regretted the words as soon as they left her mouth.

But instead of screaming, April slumped, looking sadder than Kimmie had ever seen her. "I knew you were jealous of my abilities—"

"—That's not what—"

"—but sure, you're having visions. You're talking to ghosts with your new best friend, Jenny. You've got a magic Tarot deck with disappearing cards. What next, Kimmie?"

I'm not the jealous one; she wanted to say. You're the one who always has to be the center of attention. You're the one who got upset every time I saw something you didn't.

But before she could put the words together, someone screamed.

Quinn.

✦

Quinn stumbled down the hallway in her underwear, clutching one wrist with her other hand, shivering like she'd been out in the snow. Water ran in rivulets from her hair, and she left wet footprints on the wood floor with each step. Strings of snot dripped down from her nose and clung to her chin.

April rushed to catch her as she tripped and pitched forward. Why was she wet? "We thought you and Brittany had left."

Quinn stared at her, mouth working soundlessly. She was clearly in shock.

"Let me see." April gently turned Quinn's hand, and there it was, just like Riley: the symbol Jenny had drawn in marker was now outlined in angry red welts. Like it had been branded into her skin.

She didn't understand what was happening, but she knew that Jenny was at the heart of it. April had to find a way to make her explain. Spencer would help. Unlike Kimmie, he always had her back.

She turned back to the others, who clustered behind her, watching wide-eyed.

"I think Brittany is—"

Quinn convulsed, then fell forward. Her whole body shook.

April got to her feet and raced for the room at the end of the hall, not looking back to see who followed. The door was open, and inside ...

"No."

April staggered toward Brittany — naked, curled up in a ball on her side, far too still. She touched her neck, but there was no need to feel for a pulse. Brittany's skin was cool. And purple.

And her hair was wet. What the hell?

April rolled her dead friend over. Livid bruises ringed her neck. More bruises on her breasts. And a tiny bit of red sticking out of her mouth?

Her fingers closed over it — fabric? — and pulled. It was half out of Brittany's mouth when April recognized the soggy fabric. A red silk thong.

She held it up as she glanced back at the doorway, where Spencer, Kimmie, and Toby peeked through.

Kimmie rushed in and grabbed Brittany's dress, and laid it over her. Then she turned to the two boys and said, "Give her some privacy."

April barked a laugh. "She's dead, Kimmie."

But Spencer averted his eyes respectfully. Since when did he take orders from Kimmie?

April's brother, the little creep, kept staring.

Kimmie moved to the other side of Brittany's corpse and bent over, unclenching the dead girl's fist and unfolding what had been crumpled inside.

The Three of Cups. From Sheila's Tarot deck.

No, it was Kimmie's deck now.

April stood. "We need to stick with the others. Sheila could only kill Brittany because she and Quinn were alone."

It made her feel better to say, even if she didn't believe it.

FOURTEEN

Kimmie paced while Spencer and Noah carried Quinn to the plastic-draped bed in the big room and laid her next to Riley. She didn't move after they put her down.

Riley didn't acknowledge Quinn's presence. Or that any of them returned. Catatonic? That was how Maisie's little sister ended up, didn't she?

Come to think of it, how did the sister get into the house anyway? Only one person had died. The others got out safely. Something stopped Sheila even though she didn't get all seven sacrifices.

Could it be as simple as daylight? Would sunrise banish the ghost?

Even that didn't seem hopeful. The way things were going, it was unlikely they'd last until then.

April and Toby entered the room last. April shut the door behind her, tugging it until the lock clicked.

Jenny, who'd never left, still sat with her Ouija board on her lap. She seemed lost in thought as she toyed with her pendant with one hand and tapped the planchette with the other.

April towered over Jenny, holding up her hand so that the mark was clearly visible. "What did you draw on us? What does this really mean?"

Jenny glanced up. "It's a protection symbol."

"Zach and Brittany both had it. Why didn't it protect them?"

"I have no idea."

"You didn't draw it on yourself," April accused. "Why not?"

"I told you, I have this." Jenny tapped her pendant, then laid both hands on the planchette and looked at Kimmie. "You know what we need to do to get answers."

April glared at Kimmie like it was her fault Jenny wasn't being straight with them. Then she turned back to Jenny and held out her hand.

"Give me your marker."

"What for?" Jenny asked.

"Do it," Spencer said. "Or else."

"You're not in charge of her."

Toby squared off with Spencer. Did he seriously think he could take the football player in a fight? Or was he counting on Noah to hold Spencer back?

Kimmie said to Jenny, "Just give her the marker. Please?"

That earned Kimmie another angry look from April, but at least Jenny did what April asked.

"Now take off your glove," April demanded.

Jenny shook her head, real fear glinting in her eyes. Or was it shame?

"Spencer?" April said, and the room erupted into chaos.

Jenny threw her board at Spencer's face and crawled toward the door.

Toby lunged for Spencer, swinging his fist at the side of Spencer's head.

Spencer batted the board out of the air, body-checked Toby, sending him flying, and tackled Jenny. She screamed and twisted beneath him, clawing at his face with polished black nails, but he managed to trap one arm, then the other.

Toby scrambled to his feet, but Noah grabbed him and put him in a headlock.

"April, glove," said Spencer.

Jenny spat in his face, but Spencer kept her pinned while April ripped the lace glove off her arm — revealing two rows of scarred parallel lines going all the way up, from the inside of her wrist to the inside of her elbow. And another two rows running along the back of her forearm.

Toby stopped fighting, and Noah let him go as everyone gathered around to stare.

"What the hell?" April's anger turned to shock. "Who did that to you?"

Jenny gave up fighting, tears making black trails as they leaked from the corners of her eyes.

"I did."

Cutter. Kimmie had heard that some kids did that, but she'd never seen the evidence. How long had it taken to make all those incisions? There had to be more than a hundred on each side of her arm.

What made a person hurt themselves like that?

April hesitated, then turned Jenny's hand over and used the marker to draw the protection symbol, stopping once or twice to check Spencer's to be sure she was doing it right.

Then she stood, popped the lid back on the marker, and threw it on the floor next to Jenny.

"Now, tell us what it really does," she demanded.

Spencer let Jenny go and retreated to the end of the bed. She sat up and snatched her glove off the floor and pulled it back on, covering up all those horrible scars. Then she sniffed for a moment, her dyed black hair hanging over her face.

"I told you, it's a protection symbol."

"Really? Because it doesn't seem to be doing a whole lot of protecting." April picked up Riley's branded hand and held it out toward Jenny. "Why does it turn into this?"

"I don't know." More tears slid down her cheeks, leaving dark trails behind. "None of this was supposed to happen."

"What was supposed to happen?" April asked.

"I-I just wanted to talk to her."

"About what? Sacrificing us?"

Jenny shook her head. "I didn't know. I thought it would be like a seance."

April pushed: "What did you want to talk to the ghost about?"

"Who killed her." Jenny sniffed. "I thought it would be cool to solve the mystery."

"Zach and Brittany are dead," April said. "Was it worth it?"

"Stop," Kimmie said.

Stop bullying her because you're scared; she wanted to say.

Stop blaming her because you don't want to be blamed.

Stop acting like you're in charge when you don't know any more than the rest of us do.

But none of that would make April stop; It would only make her madder.

Kimmie recognized the vicious edge of anger in her voice — from her vision of April's grandmother, library book raised overhead.

It ran in the family.

Kimmie realized that everyone was staring at her. "We can figure this out. Did Quinn kill Brittany? Or did Sheila?"

"Or did Jenny?" April said.

"I told you, she was downstairs with me." Toby's fingers fidgeted restlessly in his lap. Missing his Rubik's cube.

"Maybe you lied," April replied.

They were getting distracted again. "Fighting isn't going to solve anything."

April snorted. "Well, I guess you're in charge now, so what's your big plan for getting out of here?"

How had Kimmie never seen this mean girl side of April before? She's just afraid.

Or was It Spencer's influence?

"We already have a plan," Noah said, saving Kimmie from saying something she would regret later. "We're going back to the attic to see If we can find some tools to cut our way out of this house."

"And if that doesn't work?" April asked.

Noah ignored the question, picking the still-catatonic Quinn up from the bed and carrying her toward the door.

Kimmie took Riley's hand. "C'mon, we're going to get out of here."

But when Spencer hurried ahead to open the bedroom door, a wall of water smashed into him, knocking his body into Noah.

They both fell, disappearing into the cold, dark water that slammed into Kimmie, driving the breath out of her.

Then the water pulled her under too. She barely kept her grip on Riley's hand. She thought she heard April screaming in the distance against the undercurrent of a dull roar that could've been thousands of gallons of water rushing past.

Or maybe it was the ghost.

Phosphorescent dots. The burning in her lungs. The ice-cold pressure of the water pinning her down.

Just like in her dream.

I am dreaming. Dreams can't hurt me. Dreams aren't true.

But the screaming continued, although now she thought it was inside her head.

And underneath it, the buzzing.

Surrender, it said.

Kimmie resisted as long as she could until her lungs spasmed and her heart pounded so hard she thought it would explode.

She let the water in.

FIFTEEN

Noah came to on a soggy carpet with the taste of stagnant water in his mouth. Everything felt bruised and on fire, but at least he was alive, despite the fact that he remembered ice-cold water filling his lungs and the pressure of the water shoving him down into the dark. His tuxedo shirt and pants were soaked, plastered to his skin. His shoes squelched as he staggered to his feet.

Where was he?

Not in the Bain house, that was for sure. A Victorian gentleman's bedroom? A massive four-poster bed carved from dark wood pushed against the far wall, covered in forest green wallpaper with fussy gold accents. A fancy navy-and-gold coat on a dress mannequin that could've fit right in on the set of Pirates of the Caribbean, and a powdered wig on a wig stand on the table next to it.

A cast-iron stand containing poker, shovel, and an axe stood beside a fireplace with coals glowing — how could that be if they'd been brought here by the water?

The only window in the room was stained glass, reds, blues, greens, and yellows depicting a young man standing on a small, grassy hill, holding a sword as clouds billowed behind him. Beneath the window was a small chest of drawers carved to match the bedposts with a sword on it—a sword with a yellow gem set into the gold-chased hilt, just like its stained glass doppelgänger.

He couldn't help picking the sword up to admire it — and when his fingers touched the blade's edge, it bit into his flesh.

Hissing, he pulled his fingers away. Blood.

"Where are we?" Spencer popped over the edge of the mattress, then crawled up onto the bed. "The last thing I remember was drowning."

"Me too." Noah turned to see Quinn behind him, getting to her feet, and Toby face down beyond her. Next to him was that fucking Rubik's cube. How was that possible?

Quinn nudged Toby with her toe. He groaned and lifted his head. "Am I dead?"

Then he saw his cube and snatched it up with a smirk.

"That weed must've had something else in it," Spencer said. "I'm thinking LSD."

Toby scowled. "I see this too, and I didn't smoke anything like you degenerates did."

Even though he'd nearly drowned, the dork still had no survival instinct.

"Then someone spiked the punch," Spencer tried. "We all drank that, didn't we?"

"That was hours ago. We would've felt it much sooner." Click. Click. Spencer sneered: "How would you know? You do much LSD?"

"I'm so sick of your bullshit." Toby scrambled to his feet with a reddening face. "You think you can get away with anything because you're on the football team."

"What's your problem, nerd?"

"My problem is that you broke Kimmie's heart by dumping her because she wouldn't put out for you." Toby was spitting mad, spraying flecks of it everywhere as he yelled at Spencer. "Then you broke it again by dating her best friend. My sister. Who you'll probably dump the second she gives in to you."

"Don't act like you're her white knight. Kimmie told me all about how you've been stalking her," Spencer shot back.

Noah held up a hand. "We should—"

"Kimmie deserves better than you." Toby pointed at Noah. "Better than him."

Toby stormed toward the door and yanked on it.

It actually opened.

"Fuck you; you're all going to die anyway." Toby disappeared into what looked like a wood-paneled hallway.

Idiot. Did he think he stood a chance at facing whoever — or whatever — killed Zach and Quinn?

"We need to stay toge—" Noah called after him as the door swung shut. "We have to go after him."

"Who cares about that asshole?" Spencer asked.

"That asshole has a point," Quinn said. "Pretty shitty of you to dump Kimmie for her best friend."

"Why do you care?"

Quinn sobered. "Brittany's dead, so I can't fix what I broke there. But you can still make it right with Kimmie and April."

"Nothing to make right. Kimmie said no, and April said yes."

"But you're just playing with both of them."

"You don't know what I'm doing." Spencer's fists clenched, a sure sign that he was hitting the limits of his self-restraint.

Noah was used to watching for the fist clench at parties. It never failed — someone would rub Spencer's ego the wrong way, and he'd flip from fun mode to fight mode. And it would be Noah's job, as the not-wasted member of the group, to intervene.

He did it because that's what friends do. But that didn't mean he enjoyed it.

"Why did you break up with Brittany?" he asked Quinn. A diversion to take the attention off Spencer and give him time to cool off.

Quinn went from sober to sad. "Right before I ... blacked out, we were fighting. She was so excited about April's stupid suggestion about getting married; I didn't want to keep leading her on."

"That's what you were fighting about?" Spencer asked.

She swallowed and glanced down at the floor. "I told her I planned to break up with her when we left for college."

Ouch. Noah remembered the hopeful look on Brittany's face when April had predicted a wedding for them. She must have been crushed.

"Weren't you guys going to the same place?" Spencer asked.

"I was her first. She needed to explore, and I needed it too. And now—" Quinn's voice sounded choked. "I could've just let her think we were going to be together. At least she would've been happy before she died."

Noah screwed up his nerve in the uncomfortable silence and asked Spencer the question he'd been throttling for months.

"Why did you ask April out after you dumped Kimmie? Because you hate Kimmie or because you love April?"

Spencer sagged, looking more tired than Noah had ever seen him.

"Because you asked Kimmie out the second I dumped her," he admitted. "If I'd gone off with some other girl, we wouldn't have hung out anymore."

Ridiculous. "We'd still be friends, no matter who you're dating."

Spencer turned purple-red. "It's more than that for me."

"What do you—"

But Spencer grabbed a poker from the fireplace and stalked out the door.

"This whole time, you really didn't see it?" Quinn grabbed the axe and followed Spencer.

It had never occurred to Noah that Spencer might be into him — not the way he constantly talked about wanting to have sex with Kimmie and when that didn't pan out, with April. On the other hand ... all those double dates. Noah usually agreed because Kimmie seemed more comfortable when she was with April, and he'd thought Spencer might be suggesting they pair up because April didn't want to abandon Kimmie.

Was it possible that Spencer was the one who didn't want to be abandoned?

He looked around for a sheath to put the sword in, so he wouldn't cut himself on it, but there didn't seem to be anything like that. Should he leave the sword here?

Or should he keep it in case they ran into something that could be fought? He'd never trained with a sword, but he'd played baseball in junior high. He could at least swing it like a bat.

Holding it awkwardly upright, he yanked the door open and hurried into the dimly-lit wood-paneled hallway that seemed to go on forever in both directions, with staggered doors on both sides.

He looked left, then right, and saw Quinn and Spencer ahead. No Toby.

"Wait up!"

Running with the sword was more challenging than he'd thought because he had to hold it up and away from his body and couldn't pump his arms without fear of hurting himself. He was a little out of breath when he pulled up alongside Spencer.

"Hey, I didn't know—" That you were gay felt like the wrong thing to say. "We can still be friends, right?"

"Yeah, friends." Spencer didn't look at him.

"You know it wouldn't have bothered me if you'd told me, don't you?"

"You got all weird when I hugged you and told you I'd miss you next year."

"I wouldn't have been weird about it."

Spencer shot Noah an exasperated look, and the guilty twinge in his heart agreed.

"Okay, but I would've gotten over it."

"But the school year would've been over by then, and we wouldn't have had our best season ever."

Oh man, I suck. "I'm sorry that I wasn't the kind of friend you could trust to tell something like that."

"Nothing would've happened anyway. I'm bi; you're very very straight—"

"When you say it like that, it sounds like an insult."

Spencer smiled just a little, and Noah thought they might be okay after all.

"Hey, do you hear that?" Quinn stopped so fast that Noah had to swing the sword away to avoid stabbing her. He gulped and took a couple of steps back.

"It's coming from there." Spencer pointed to a door farther down the hallway.

Now Noah could hear the faint sound of someone pounding on the door and yelling.

Toby.

◆

Toby's hands ached from pounding on the door, and his throat was sore from yelling. The water was up to his knees, numbing every inch of skin it touched but making the flesh underneath throb with pain.

He wished he'd stayed with the others. Thrown the Rubik's cube at Spencer's face and taken the pounding he would've gotten before Noah pulled Spencer off of him.

Except that he hated Noah too, for always being the one to rescue him.

And he hated himself for always needing to be rescued.

But the worst part was that he was starting to hate Kimmie for not realizing how much better she could've had it if she'd said yes to him instead of to the first guy who asked her out after Spencer dumped her.

If only he'd gotten there first. He could've been the one whose shoulder she cried on. The one who told her she was pretty and that anyone who dumped her was an idiot.

But by the time he'd planned out how he was going to ask her — and convinced Grandma Patricia to give him money for chocolate and flowers — Noah had taken possession of Kimmie.

His Kimmie.

If Kimmie had waited a little longer for Toby, they wouldn't be here.

Toby wouldn't have had to find another date for prom, just for the privilege of being with Kimmie on the biggest night of senior year. He'd thought it would be worth it, even if he had to watch her constantly dancing with Noah.

But it wasn't.

And if Toby hadn't been desperate enough to ask Jenny, an outsider he'd met in DMs through the Zombie Hunter guild he gamed with, they never would've used the Ouija board to wake up Sheila. Toby couldn't have cared less about Jenny, but taking her side against April was fun whenever psychic stuff got brought up. Except for Toby, no one ever had the guts to tell April that her Tarot readings were bullshit.

And he'd thought that, while April was fighting with Jenny and Noah was trying to make peace, he might manage to take Kimmie aside and tell her how he felt.

Instead, they'd been trapped in a legitimately haunted house, which had driven Kimmie into Noah's arms for real. They were probably all going to die, and if you really thought about it; this was all Kimmie's fault.

If they managed to get out of here, he would have to explain it to her and make sure that nothing like this ever happened again.

No, not if. When. It was on him to find a way out and get back to the house, so he could find a way to rescue Kimmie.

Or at least, so they could die together. If that were the closest he could get to being with her, he'd take it.

The water was waist-deep now. He fought his growing panic as he banged on the door again, in case those other idiots were nearby to hear.

Toby thought he was drowning before, but then he'd woken up here, which suggested that maybe he wasn't actually here: his body could be back at Sheila's house while he hallucinated this insane mansion that looked like it belonged on Downton Abbey.

Besides, what was the other explanation? That Sheila had magically teleported them somewhere else? That they'd somehow wandered into a parallel dimension?

More likely, he'd hallucinate drowning again and wake up back at the actual house, with Kimmie and the others.

I should drown myself and get it over with.

He was about to drop down into the dark, swirling water and inhale deeply when he heard someone pounding on the door from the other side.

"Toby, are you in there?"

Quinn the least objectionable one in the group. She'd never bullied or patronized him when she could tear herself away from Brittany long enough to reply to something Toby had said.

"It's no use. The door's locked, and the water's up to my chest."

"Stand back."

There was a thud. Then another. And his side of the door started to splinter as an axe blade penetrated the wood.

But the water was nearly up to his chin. And it wasn't real anyway. It was time for him to be a man and get back to Kimmie faster.

Toby let himself fall into the water's icy embrace.

Then he took a breath.

KING of PENTACLES

SIXTEEN

Kimmie retched herself awake, throwing up fetid water and bile as she pushed her head up, making a puddle on the … crimson shag carpet? Where was she?

She blinked away tears and sat up. The room was massive, and horned animal heads were mounted on the walls. Different types of bulls, she thought. Was that one a water buffalo? An ox? A yak?

At the far end of the room sat a huge golden throne, and on one side of it, a padlocked chest that would have been perfect for stashing a pirate's treasure. On the other side stood a small pillar holding a platter piled high with grapes. A long curved bull's horn rested point down in a metal holder next to the platter — a drinking horn, like in movies about Vikings.

Then she noticed she was clutching the Tarot deck in one hand. How had she managed to hang onto that, but not to Riley?

Someone groaned behind her.

Kimmie turned to see Riley struggling to sit up, looking just as dazed as Kimmie felt. Beyond Riley, April sprawled face up, and Jenny face down. Neither of them moved.

A sick feeling of dread settled in her stomach.

I am dreaming. Dreams can't hurt me. Dreams aren't true.

Once, that mantra had comforted her. But she was starting to think that her therapist had lied to her. Because this dream was hurting her, and it felt as true as anything she'd ever experienced.

"What the hell happened?" Riley asked, her voice weak and thready. "Are we dead?"

Kimmie's lungs burned like she had actually inhaled water. Her skin was cold and numb. And she was drenched from head to toe. But she was still breathing. Would a spirit need to breathe?

"I don't think so."

Riley turned her head and whimpered as she saw one of the bull-heads on the wall. She scrambled to her feet. Whirled around. "It's happening again."

"Is this the room where you and Zach were before?"

Riley shook her head frantically. "I've never been here before!"

"Where are we?" April asked, making squishy sounds as she got to her feet. Her shimmery red dress clung to her breasts, her hips — parting to reveal one long, bare leg — and Kimmie forgot everything else for a moment. Even half-drowned, April was beautiful. "What is this?"

April walked over to the small table picked up the drinking horn, and looked inside it. "Empty."

Jenny startled awake and spat. The water had caused her makeup to run in black and pink smears, like war paint. Part of her skirt had ripped off, leaving her lopsided. She got to her feet, and her mouth fell open.

"Holy shit," she said. "King of Pentacles."

"What?" April stopped wringing out her hair to glare at Jenny. "What are you babbling about?"

"That's the card you drew for Riley, wasn't it?"

"So?"

"So—" Jenny pointed to each of the items as she named them. "—the throne, the four bulls, the grapes, the literal fucking treasure chest. King of Pentacles. Where's your deck, April?"

"Somehow, I forgot to grab it while I was drowning."

"I have Sheila's." Kimmie searched through the deck. Found the King of Pentacles. Held it up. "She's right."

Riley started hyperventilating, stuffing a fist against her mouth. "Oh god, I'm going to die, just like Zach. And my baby's going to die too."

"It's okay." April only meant to hug Riley, but the other girl latched onto her and wouldn't let go. She trembled as she cried in April's arms.

Kimmie tried the door. "We're locked in."

Riley wailed.

✦

Water poured through the hole in the door as Quinn continued to hack at it with the axe. Beside her, Spencer jabbed at the splintered wood with the wrought-iron poker, clearing out the debris.

Noah stood with the dumb sword, afraid to swing it at the door and risk hurting his friends. Why hadn't he grabbed something more practical?

It didn't make sense to try the other doors and risk getting separated from the others. The best he could do was stand guard, watching for anything approaching from either direction. Praying that nothing would come.

"Toby, say something!" Quinn yelled.

But Toby didn't answer, and Noah couldn't see light coming through the hole, just more water pouring out. Were they too late? Or was he treading water as it continued to rise to the ceiling?

Except for the water gushing through the hole in the door, the hallway was dry—none of this made sense. The doors couldn't possibly be watertight, but somehow nothing leaked through the edges between the door and its frame or the gap between the door and carpet.

And where was it coming from? If he hadn't been careful tonight — a single puff from Zach's joint, a beer while they were doing the Ouija board — he'd have agreed with Spencer that this had to be a drug-induced hallucination.

But even if there'd been LSD in the joint, he couldn't explain where the gun that had killed Zach had come from, why his clothes were drenched, or why everyone's hallucinations were apparently the same.

A cracking sound reverberated through the hallway, shaking the floor. Quinn and Spencer stopped hacking at the door as Noah stepped backward to keep his balance.

Then the door bulged outward, the wood splintering around the hole.

"It's going to break!" Quinn yelled, backing away.

"We have to get out of here!" Spencer grabbed her arm and ran down the hall.

Noah dropped his sword and turned to follow, but the door exploded outward, sending a wall of water crashing into him and sweeping him down the hallway in the opposite direction.

He fought against the current, but it was too strong. It yanked him under the surface, farther away from his friends. A doorframe rammed into his spine as the water swept him into another room. He flailed his arms, trying to grab something — anything — to keep from being pulled farther under. But his hands closed on nothing.

The water was so cold it burned his skin, and he could feel his body going into shock. His vision grayed around the edges as he felt himself losing consciousness.

Then gray became black.

THE HERMIT

SEVENTEEN

April hugged Riley tighter and rocked her like a little kid, but she kept sobbing. April wasn't sure how long they'd been stuck here, but she was sick of listening to Kimmie bonding with her new best friend Jenny as they searched for hidden doors and secret panels in the walls.

"But how can we be hallucinating?" Kimmie asked. "Everything here feels so solid. My clothes are wet. If I was hallucinating, wouldn't they be dry?"

Jenny shook her head. "Sheila was a psychic, not a witch. But even if she was a witch, I've never heard of someone being able to conjure actual matter out of nothing."

"So it's more like a dream, where impossible things happen that break the laws of physics, but your mind just accepts it?"

"Except we're all having the same dream, and you can die in it."

"How do we wake up?" Kimmie asked. "If we find a way out of the house, will that do it?"

Jenny shrugged. "Maybe Sheila put a spell on the house before she died. To curse anyone who came inside."

April couldn't help butting in. "I thought you said she was a psychic, not a witch."

But even as she said the words, April remembered the way the door had slammed shut behind them, then the water rushing in. There was no other explanation for what was happening. Was there?

None of the books she'd read contained anything remotely helpful for this situation. They were all about meditating to get into an alpha state, clearly visualizing what you wanted, and listening to your intuition. Rituals with crystals and other pretty things.

There hadn't been a single thing about protecting yourself from murderous ghosts. Or drowning in a magical flood. Or being stabbed in the back by your best friend who suddenly wanted to be a psychic. Just a lot of blah blah blah about setting intentions and making sure you were thinking about the highest good for all involved.

April felt betrayed. If she survived this, she was going to track down every one of those authors and tell them what frauds they were.

Riley's sobbing subsided into soft whimpers, but April kept rocking her. Even though her shoulder was wet with tears and probably snot, given how hard Riley had been ugly-crying. Not that it mattered at this point what she had on her. Her prom dress — the dress she'd spent half a year's allowance on — was utterly ruined.

Jenny owed her a prom dress. And a new best friend.

"I want Zach," Riley whispered. "I want him back."

"I'm sorry," April whispered.

Jenny knocked on another panel, cocking her head. Could she really tell the difference between a secret door and a solid wall, or was she tapping on everything because that's what people did in movies?

April had never hated anyone more than she hated Jenny right now.

And not just because she'd ruined April's plan with her stupid Ouija board and her ghost-summoning candle. Sheila might have woken up and attacked them anyway.

She didn't hate Jenny because she'd claimed that April was a fraud and that Kimmie was the one with psychic powers. However, that was an excellent reason to loathe her.

The real reason she hated Jenny right now was because of the way Kimmie looked at her. She looked at Jenny the way she used to look at April — like she was the most important person in the universe. The person who was going to explain everything, so it made sense.

If April was going to be murdered by a ghost, Kimmie should at least have the decency to keep being her best friend until after she was dead.

Because without Kimmie, April had no one.

And that was a fate worse than death.

＋

Kimmie knocked on another wall panel, casting a sideways glance at Jenny. She couldn't stop thinking about the scars hiding under the glove April had taken off her. And wondering if there were similar scars on the other arm.

"What?" Jenny asked.

Kimmie swallowed, her mouth suddenly dry. Should she ask? It wasn't like they hadn't all seen them.

"Those scars you gave yourself," she said. "Why?"

Jenny knocked on another panel before answering. "I wanted to kill myself, but I didn't have the guts. So I did that instead."

What had happened to Jenny that had been terrible enough to make her think about suicide?

"Do you still want to die?" she asked.

"Not today."

Jenny tapped on another panel. They all sounded the same to Kimmie, although she'd never admit that to April. It felt futile, but they had to get out of here somehow, and she didn't have any other ideas.

Maybe this was like an escape room; she was supposed to collect clues. The animal heads. The throne. The grapes. She knew they were all from the Tarot card, but what did they mean?

"How long have you known you had the gift?" Jenny asked.

Kimmie glanced at April, who was talking to Riley in a soft, soothing voice. April was already mad at her for 'taking Jenny's side.' The last thing she wanted was to start another fight.

"I don't believe in that psychic stuff," she said.

"But you've had visions. Known things you shouldn't have? Dreamed things before they happened?"

"How did you know?"

"Because I knew someone once who had it too, and her aura was the same as yours."

"You read auras?" Another thing Kimmie didn't believe in. "Seriously, you're just making all this up."

"She didn't understand her gift, and she died." Jenny tapped on the same panel she'd tapped on a moment ago. "If you have the same gift, you must learn how to us it, before it uses you."

"I don't want it. I want to live my normal life and be happy."

Jenny sighed. "Sometimes life—"

"—doesn't give you a choice," Kimmie finished. "I don't believe that."

"Sooner or later, you will."

Kimmie stole another glance at April, who was either absorbed in talking to Riley or completely ignoring Kimmie. Probably the latter.

She turned back to Jenny. "Why did you agree to come to prom with Toby tonight? You don't like him, do you?"

"I barely know him." Tap tap tap. "I wanted to see if Sheila would talk to us."

"Why?"

"Because she was a real psychic who'd developed her powers to a high degree. Her knowledge was lost when she died."

"Yet she didn't know she was going to die," Kimmie pointed out. "So her powers didn't do her much good."

"Maybe she knew it was coming, but she couldn't stop it."

Jenny sounded so sure of herself; It pissed Kimmie off. "Stop it. Stop trying to scare me."

"I'm just telling you the truth."

Kimmie knocked on the next panel so hard she hurt her knuckles. "The truth is that we need to get out of this room."

She checked on April again. April's back was to Kimmie and Jenny, although the way her head was tilted, Kimmie would've bet that April was listening to their conversation as she patted Riley on the back.

"You're not doing her any favors by lying to her," Jenny said. "About her powers. Or... the other thing."

"I'm not lying about anything." But of course, her stupid face gave her away by turning hot.

Jenny gave her a don't bullshit me look.

Kimmie wanted to slap Jenny but forced herself to turn back to the wall and rap on the next panel instead.

The important thing was to get back to the others.

Then they could figure out the real reason this was happening.

WHEEL of FORTUNE

EIGHTEEN

Use the cards. The buzzy voice wouldn't stop ordering Kimmie around, no matter how hard she tried to ignore it.

She knocked on another panel and listened. She didn't know how a secret door was supposed to sound, but everywhere she knocked sounded the same, and the whole wall couldn't be one big secret door … could it?

"Uh, guys?" April said. "It's starting again."

Before Kimmie could turn around, she felt water wash over her feet, numbing them instantly. That was another thing that didn't make sense — how could the water be so cold? Like it came from beneath the ice of a frozen lake instead of the river that ran through town.

Right, that's the part of this that doesn't make sense.

Jenny ran to the not-so-secret door and tried it again. Still locked. "Fuck!"

Sheila's deck practically vibrated against Kimmie's fingers. It just made her miss her cell phone more. One phone call and this would all be over — if only her phone still worked, if only it had even one little bar, if only she could get back to the Bain house and find it. She would take any punishment if this night could be over.

Use the cards.

The water crept up her calves, moving faster now. She should give in and let herself drown again. There was a chance she'd wake up somewhere else. Someplace perhaps less dangerous. Maybe in reality? She'd be ecstatic to wake up on that rotted couch in Sheila's parlor and see the pink light of sunrise streaming through the filthy windows and gleaming off all those dumb crystals.

Jenny threw herself against the door. Trying to break it down. But she bounced off so hard she lost her balance and fell.

Use the cards.

With a sigh, Kimmie unclenched the fist holding Sheila's deck and started flipping through it, hoping the voice would tell her what to do with the cards. Four of Cups. Ten of Wands. Temperance. Seven of Swords. The Devil. The Wheel.

As her fingers touched the Wheel card, the buzz in her head crescendoed. She held the card up to Jenny. "What does this one mean?"

"Seriously?" April said. "You're doing a reading now?"

Jenny quickly glanced at the card before she got to her feet and started kicking the door right next to the handle. BAM!

Good thing she was the kind of girl who wore combat boots with her prom dress.

"Cycles of destiny." BAM!

"Circumstances are solving your problems for you." BAM!

"Events that are bigger than you." BAM!

"What about when it's reversed?" Kimmie asked as Jenny lined herself up for another kick.

"Adversity that can only be endured. Or things taking a huge turn for the worse."

BAM!

April laughed bitterly. "We're so screwed."

The Wheel turns, the voice buzzed. Use it.

"The voice says that the Wheel turns and we can use it," Kimmie said. "What does that mean?"

Jenny thought as the water rose from Kimmie's hips to her waist.

"This room is decorated with the elements from the King of Pentacles," she finally said. "What if this place is some sort of psychic projection, and Sheila is using the cards to imagine it?"

"Like a house of Tarot?" Kimmie asked.

"You're psychic too. It's possible that you can change the projection?"

"You mean, visualize the card?" April asked.

"Exactly." Jenny nodded at April, then turned back to Kimmie. "Why don't you see if you can redecorate?"

Then she kicked the door again.

The card vibrated against her fingers. Kimmie couldn't help wondering if the deck could be alive. Or was it her ability that created the vibration and the buzzy voice?

No time to wonder — the water lapped at her ribcage. In less than a minute, she'd probably drown again.

And while she'd woken up the last time, what were the odds that she'd survive again?

She stared intently at the card, memorizing the wheel at the center, with a sphinx on top and winged creatures on clouds at each corner: angel, bird, cow, and ...was that a lion?

She closed her eyes and reimagined the room: ahead of her, a massive water wheel like the one they'd seen on their school trip to the old mill, mounted against the wall where the throne sat now, so tall that she had to raise the ceiling.

At the center of the water wheel, she imagined a big disk with a painting of the Sphinx from Egypt.

Did the water drop a little bit?

Yes, it had been up to her bra, but now it was halfway down her ribs.

She focused harder, scrunching her eyes as she imagined the animal heads disappearing. She replaced them with floating marble statues of the four-winged creatures on big cottony clouds. They came out cartoony, but at least they were friendly-looking.

"It's working!" Jenny yelled.

After fixing the image in her mind — something she'd learned to do while meditating with April years ago — she opened her eyes.

It was real—the water wheel with the sphinx, the floating statues.

As the wheel turned, it scooped up water, but when the water got up to the top, it must've gone somewhere else because the sections came back down again, empty.

It should've been impossible, but who cared?

"This doesn't make any sense." April waded closer, half-dragging Riley with her, carrying the drinking horn in her free hand. "Where is the water going?"

"Who cares?" Jenny said. "At least we're not going to drown."

"But we could be stuck here forever," April complained.

Jenny turned to Kimmie. "If you can imagine the rest of the room, maybe you can imagine that the door opens. This isn't Sheila's room anymore; It's yours."

Could it be that simple?

Kimmie imagined walking to the door, turning the knob, and hearing the latch click as she pulled the door open.

Then she nodded at Jenny, who slogged through the water — only up to Kimmie's thighs now — and opened the door.

The water rushed out faster than it had flooded in, knocking Jenny down as it pushed her through the door. Kimmie stumbled and fell as the water sucked her feet out from under her.

As the water closed over her head, she relaxed, holding her breath and letting the current carry her toward the door. As she floated, she made up a new mantra.

This is my dream. Dreams can't hurt me unless I let them. I decide if this dream is true.

The water dumped her onto carpet, then receded, leaving her soaking wet in a puddle, but like before, the rest of the carpet was dry.

Jenny lay face up on the other side of the room — the second-floor bedroom where she and Noah had been making out earlier. The candle she'd lit earlier still flickered, although it was more than half gone by now.

She'd done it. She'd fought back against Sheila and won. For once, there was a good side to the power she'd been cursed with.

She kissed the Wheel card, then tucked it back into the deck.

A door slammed behind her. She turned, ready for a fight, but Sheila wasn't there. The room was empty, except for Kimmie and Jenny.

Wait.

Where were April and Riley?

ACE OF SWORDS

NINETEEN

Noah rolled over and half-coughed, half-vomited dank water onto the stained wooden floor. Pain exploded through his head; a pulsing agony made him wish he could pass out again. He reached up to touch the back of his head and found a throbbing lump. It reminded him of when he'd ended up under a pile of three linebackers and had to spend the night in the hospital with a broken arm and a concussion.

He looked up weakly and saw auras around the moonlight slanting in through small smeary dormer windows — the storm outside seemed to have passed. The dusty floor around him was spattered with fat, wet splotches, and the air smelled like dead mice. Attic, he thought dimly. The water must've brought me back.

But unlike the first time he'd been transported — and nearly drowned — he didn't see the others nearby. Were they still at the other place, trying to swim to safety? Or had they been taken elsewhere?

Maybe they were downstairs, waiting for him to join them.

Or maybe they were never coming back because they were dead. Because he'd failed to save them.

Bile rose in his throat, and he had to swallow hard to keep from being sick again. He definitely had a concussion.

He tried to stand, but his legs were rubbery and would barely support him. He leaned against the wall and made his way slowly to the stairs, pausing every few steps to catch his breath.

It would've been so easy to lie back down and sleep. Just for a few minutes.

He rested his forehead against the wall as he gathered the strength to take the first step. When he was finally ready to start moving downward, he clutched the railing to keep from losing his balance.

A metallic stench hit him as he stepped off the last stair onto the second-floor landing. He squinted through the blur at something gleaming in the moonlight from the window at the end of the hall. He cautiously edged closer to get a better look.

The sword. Crimson stained the blade.

The room tilted around him. He put out a hand to steady himself against the wall and closed his eyes, taking deep breaths and willing the vertigo to pass.

"Is that you, Noah?" It sounded like Spencer, his voice hoarse. He cleared his throat, coughing a little. Noah guessed that he was at the far end of the hall, where it was too dark for Noah to see without a flashlight.

Noah took a step forward and tripped as his foot hit something. He fell hard, hitting the floor with a jarring thud that spiked the pain in his head. He vomited again, arching upward to keep his face out of the noxious puddle.

His hand squelched into something warm and sticky as he struggled to sit up. He yanked his hand back and held it up in the moonbeam—blood, same as the crimson on the sword.

"Shit!" Whose blood was it?

He groped until he found an arm, and followed it down to a wrist. Then he scooted himself backward, a few inches at a time until he'd dragged her far enough into the moonlight to see Quinn's face, mouth slack, eyes staring glassily at nothing.

He dragged her further, revealing a massive bloodstain on her white shirt, sliced open over her belly button. Noah parted the fabric with trembling hands. A gaping wound, still welling fresh blood.

Spencer crawled out of the darkness on hands and knees. His shirt and pants were stained with blood.

Quinn's blood.

"What did you do?" Noah cried.

"Nothing." Spencer sat up. He shook like a frightened puppy, hugging himself. "The door broke. We got washed away. And I woke up here, with that—"

He pointed to the bloody sword, then froze, staring at the back of his hand. Noah grabbed Spencer's wrist and brought it closer until he could see it clearly through his concussed blur. Jenny's symbol now looked like it had been branded on him.

Spencer swore. "I don't remember anything else."

Noah bit back the scream of rage and fear that roiled in his throat. He'd been ready to believe that Riley had killed Zach accidentally, then hid the gun. Or lost track of it while she was in shock.

He could understand Quinn being so angry with Brittany that she'd accidentally strangled her and that the guilt was so horrible she'd blotted it out.

But you didn't stab someone by accident. Or did you? Noah had lost his grip on the sword when the water knocked him down. Could it have driven the blade through Quinn as it swept them down the hallway, impaling her like one of those videos where a tornado would drive a piece of straw through a wooden fence post?

But if that was what happened, would Spencer be covered in blood? Probably not.

Which meant Spencer had killed Quinn.

But Noah didn't see how he could've shot Zach and tricked Riley into thinking she'd done it.

He could've strangled Brittany, however. But if he'd snuck into their room, why wouldn't Quinn have said so? She genuinely seemed to believe that she did it. And April would've had to cover for him.

None of this made sense. But it seemed impossible to deny that his friends were murdering each other, one by one.

He did scream then, triggering another spike of agony in his head so intense that he blacked out for a moment, and when he came too, it was in mid-retch as his stomach convulsed, spewing out more bile.

Footsteps on the creaky stairs below, then Toby appeared on the landing. "What—"

Noah spit to clear his mouth. "I think Spencer killed Quinn. With that sword."

He pointed to the floor behind him, but the sword was gone.

TWENTY

Jenny narrowed her eyes in annoyance, muttering something Kimmie couldn't quite hear, then spun around and darted out into the hallway.

Kimmie reached for her. "Wait, where are you going?"

She followed, nearly running into her when Jenny stopped short, a small surprised yelp escaping from her as she brought her hands up to her mouth to muffle a scream.

Kimmie looked down to see Noah, his back turned to her and

kneeling near a pool of vomit on the rotten carpet. He stood slowly up and turned towards her, and she saw that his tux pants were spattered with it.

His face was bloodless, and pale, like he was in shock. He opened his mouth to say something, but nothing came out.

Spencer was there too. Crouched against the wall, he was holding his head in his hands. His white shirt was splotched with fresh blood stains, and she could hear him moaning. "No, no, no ...."

Toby stood at the top of the stairs, looking back and forth at the scene's terrible details, his mouth hanging open. He looked down, and Kimmie followed his gaze to where she had been instinctively avoiding looking.

Quinn, her corpse, torso soaked in blood. Her belly was torn open, sliced by a massive stab wound, and guts spilled out on the floor.

The smell hit her, overwhelming and terrible, and Kimmie braced herself against the wall and threw up.

Noah managed to stumble over to her, bracing her shoulder and holding her hair back as she convulsed until there was nothing left.

"I d-d-didn't do it. She was like that when I woke up." Spencer pointed a shaking finger at Toby. "But he came back before we did."

"I just woke up downstairs!" Toby sounded defensive, complaining.

"Or you found us both unconscious, and you stabbed Quinn. You're only pretending you just woke up."

Toby came up into the hallway and glared down his nose at Spencer. "What do you think I stabbed her with?"

"You found the sword." Spencer looked around wildly. "Where did it go?"

Kimmie's earlier vision returned to her. Quinn on the floor, her face contorted in terror, her crisp white shirt and the front of her pants soaked in blood.

What card had April drawn for Quinn? Ace of Swords, wasn't it? And Quinn had been stabbed by a sword.

Hands trembling, she pulled Sheila's deck from her pocket and fanned through the deck, searching for the card.

It wasn't there.

Why no Tarot card this time when there'd been one next to each of the other bodies?

With sudden resolve, she grabbed Jenny by the arm. "Help me roll her over."

Jenny's eyes flashed but faded into resignation. She moved to the corpse's side, and together with Kimmie, they rolled her over.

She was strangely heavy. It felt like she was filled with wet sand.

Maybe that's what happens when your soul leaves your body, Kimmie thought. Without it, you're just deadweight.

There was a card underneath Quinn's shoulder. Facedown. Kimmie was afraid to look because of what it might mean, but she had to know.

Flipping it over, she held it up. It was reversed, the way she was looking at it—a disembodied hand, stabbed down with a single, massive blade: the Ace of Swords.

Noah looked at it over her shoulder. "Who had access to that deck?"

He sounded ... suspicious?

Noah didn't think that she'd killed Quinn, did he?

✦

Noah stared at Quinn's corpse. Now what?

He glanced at Kimmie, who leaned against the wall, whispering with Jenny. April had retreated to the top step of the stairs and sat next to Toby, although she was as far away as she could be from him and still share the step.

Spencer sat with his forehead on his knees and his arms around both legs.

Noah's vision swam, then cleared again. He had to get everyone moving again, not because there was someplace to go, but because if they all sank into shock, they wouldn't be able to fight back when the next bad thing happened.

And more bad things were definitely going to happen.

Noah nudged Spencer gently with his toe.

Spencer raised his head, but he frowned like he wasn't sure what to do next.

"Help me move Quinn," said Noah. "She should be with Brittany."

He nodded grimly, picking her body up under the arms. Noah gripped her ankles and lifted. They carried the body down the hall to the bedroom at the end, trying not to look at her as they walked.

"I swear, I don't remember anything after the water hit us." Spencer started walking backward. "I just remember choking on it; then I passed out."

"I believe you." He had to because if he thought Spencer had meant to kill Quinn, he would lose his shit right now.

"I don't know how I got the sword."

"I said I believe you."

Spencer sped up a beat, probably anxious to get this over with.

Noah struggled to keep up, and his grip slipped, and he dropped one of Quinn's ankles. Her leg hit the ground heavily, jerking the body. Dark liquid gushed from the stab wound, splashing on the floor.

Noah clenched his teeth, trying not to throw up at the sheer nastiness of the job they were doing. The smell, the feeling of handling a corpse.

"I can drag her the rest of the way," said Spencer.

"She doesn't deserve that." She didn't deserve to die, either. And Noah didn't deserve to carry her corpse around a haunted house.

None of them deserved any of this.

"You need to rest," Spencer said.

Noah grunted as he picked up the ankle he'd dropped. "We're almost there."

They started walking again. Spencer took baby steps to make it easier for Noah. When they got to the last room, Spencer kicked the door all the way open so they could shuffle inside.

The bedroom was dimly lit by the candle that had been there earlier, which had burned down less than Noah would've expected. So much was happening, in such a short time.

The candle flickered unsteadily, making his head spin and his stomach churn. His headache shifted from a fiery ache to a deep, stabbing pain.

They managed to lower Quinn next to Brittany's half naked corpse. Brittany was still partially covered in her prom dress still staring blankly at the ceiling, looking for an answer to why this had happened to her.

The pain in his skull, nausea, and vertigo all added up to too much. He lurched over to the corner of the bedroom and spewed acid and bile uncontrollably through his mouth and nose. His sinuses burned, adding another layer of pain to his headache. He wanted nothing more than to sit down, to just lie down, to just rest a few minutes.

But his heart was pounding with terror at the thought: if I fall asleep, I will die.

Wake up. Breathing heavily, he wiped his mouth and nose and turned around.

"Do you believe that a ghost is possessing us?" Spencer asked.

"Would you rather believe," said Noah, trying to concentrate, "that we're taking turns murdering each other and lying about it?"

"No." But something in his expression made Noah wonder if Spencer would rather think his friends were murderers than believe in ghosts.

Then: "I thought maybe it was Toby. I've always thought he was a serial killer in the making."

"Is that why you're always on his case?" Spencer didn't seem to have an answer for that, but talking was distracting him from wanting to sleep, so Noah continued, lowering his voice so the others in the hallway wouldn't hear. "This whole thing is Jenny's fault. If we get out of here, we need to make sure the sheriff understands that."

"Out of all of us, I thought you'd be the one to insist we tell the truth."

"And trade my football scholarship for a spot in an insane asylum?"

Noah shook his head, then wished he hadn't because the room kept moving when he stopped. "We need to get our stories straight. You talk to April, and I'll talk to Kimmie. If the four of us say something that makes sense, it won't matter what Jenny and Toby say."

"What about Toby?" Spencer asked. "If he sides with us, it's everyone else against Jenny."

"We can't trust Toby."

Not because he'd brought Jenny – it was clear they barely knew each other. They couldn't trust Toby because he was obsessed with Kimmie. Toby would do anything if he thought it would make him a hero to her.

Spencer sighed. "He's a nerdy creep, but does he deserve to go to jail because he was desperate enough to ask the wrong girl to prom?"

"Better him than all of us, right?"

KING OF PENTACLES

TWENTY-ONE

The house shook. A loud double thump came from overhead. It sounded like the floor above. Had someone fallen? Kimmie bolted to the staircase leading into the attic.

Halfway up, she quickly looked back and saw the others following her. Noah was bringing up the rear, holding his head and looking ready to fall over. Wincing in sympathy and worry, she turned and continued up the steps.

An unholy sight greeted her in the attic.

Sheila, a glowing apparition, her limbs wreathed in cold, flickering blue flames, her white gown fluttering in a slow liquid breeze that none of them could feel.

She floated in the center of the room, holding a Viking drinking horn that gleamed with silver light. Numbly, Kimmie thought: from the King of Pentacle's room.

A huddled lump of wet rags shivered at Sheila's feet. Riley, on her hands and knees, a soaked dress dirtier and more torn than the last time Kimmie had seen her.

Riley was shivering and making whimpering noises. She looked up, and a tiny flicker of hope crossed her features. "Help me," she gasped.

Sheila looked up, and her eyes locked with Kimmie,; she somehow knew Instantly what the ghost intended.

Her hand struck like a snake, grabbing Riley by her hair and jerking her up to her feet with a strength that nearly broke her neck. She struggled, but Sheila's grip was like a vice, unmoving as she tried to escape.

Her other hand raised the drinking horn, and Kimmie saw its sharp tip, saw a sigil burning on the back of her hand with an intense blue flame. With a shock, she realized it was the same protection symbol that Jenny had inscribed on the backs of their hands.

With a swift motion, Sheila stabbed the tip of the horn into the side of Riley's throat.

"No!" Kimmie screamed.

Behind her, Spencer swore, and Noah made a sick sound, a helpless cry of anguish.

Jenny gasped. Sheila caught the hot stream of blood in the mouth of the drinking horn as Jenny slumped to the ground.

Sheila smiled at Kimmie, winked, and toasted them with the drinking horn, bringing it to her lips. As she did so, the apparition faded, and she saw April emerge from the fading glow, one hand tangled in Riley's hair, the other holding the horn to her lips.

"April!" shouted Spencer.

April gasped, letting go of Riley's hair and dropping the drinking horn to the ground, spilling blood everywhere. The crimson liquid glazed her lips.

In a daze, she looked at Riley bleeding out on the floor, at the drinking horn spilling blood. She looked at the back of her hand, seeing the fading glow of the symbol, and fainted next to Riley.

Kimmie ran forward to try to stanch the flow of blood with the skirt of her dress, but the wound was a horrible jagged hole in her neck.

Riley looked up at her, her mouth opening and closing as air bubbled from the wound and blood foamed from her mouth, trying to say something.

But it was hopeless. Kimmie watched helplessly as Riley died.

Soaked in her blood, Kimmie collapsed across her body, weeping.

Jenny had knelt next to April and was trying to shake her away. Spencer, a few steps behind, joined her. He used his shirt to wipe the blood from her mouth.

"Come on, baby. Come on, wake up, April." He looked at Jenny, his gaze saying, keep trying.

Spencer picked up the drinking horn. The tip was sharp and slick with blood. More blood drooled from it onto the floor as he held it.

Somehow, Kimmie pulled herself together, and drew herself up from Riley's corpse. She saw on the floor, a card: the King of Pentacles. She picked it up, and put it in her pocket, knowing it was undoubtedly Sheila's and that it would be missing if she looked through the deck.

"Kimmie," said Jenny, getting her attention.

She was aware, in retrospect that Jenny had been calling her name repeatedly. Kimmie turned around, and Jenny held up April's wrist to show her the back of her hand. The protective symbol was burned like a brand into her skin. What did it mean?

"April killed Riley," Spencer whispered, still holding the drinking horn and taking a step back as he stared at her unconscious form.

"Sheila killed Riley." Kimmie stood, wiping her bloody hands on her even bloodier skirt. "It wasn't April."

"Possession," Jenny said. "Sheila's collecting her sacrifices through us."

Spencer shook his head. "It was April. I saw her."

"Kimmie saw Sheila because Kimmie's psychic. You're not, so you saw April. Sheila was controlling her."

"I saw April kill Riley. With this." Spencer raised one hand — it was empty. "The fuck?"

Click.

Toby sat on a box under the eaves, hands fussing with his Rubik's cube as he calmly watched them. "No one has died when we've stayed together, only when two of us have gone off alone."

"So as long as we don't pair up—" Jenny started.

"Exactly."

Click.

"Why can't Sheila possess one of us when we're in a group?" Spencer asked.

Everyone looked at Jenny, who shrugged. "Maybe she can, but she hasn't yet. I don't know; I don't make the rules."

Kimmie wondered who did.

April groaned and started to roll over. "Why does my—"

She came nose to nose with Riley and screamed, scrambling backward to flee her friend's corpse, stopping only when she slammed into the wall.

She raised her hand to point at Riley, then stopped to gape at the brand seared into it.

Then she screamed again.

THE HEIROPHANT

TWENTY-TWO

April writhed as she spit out nasty-tasting water on the rough wood floor. Through watering eyes, she saw the line near her hand and realized she was back in the attic. In the center of the pentagram. Blinking to clear her stinging tears, she saw a black stiletto-heeled boot a few feet away.

Riley.

Relief flooded through her. The last thing she remembered was clutching the horn of the water buffalo head mounted on the wall of that stupid room with one hand while she supported an unconscious Riley with the other as the water neared the ceiling.

Poor Riley had some kind of panic attack about the time the water got to their shoulders. She'd hyperventilated until she'd passed out.

As she struggled to get up, Kimmie appeared between April and Riley and lifted April into a sitting position. April clung to her for a moment, gasping for air, then tried to look over Kimmie's shoulder at Riley.

But Kimmie shifted just enough to block April's view.

"Is Riley breathing?" she asked. "As soon as you left, the water wheel disappeared, and the room started to fill up again."

Horror flashed across Kimmie's face. "Oh god, I should've gone last; I didn't realize—"

"None of us realized." How could they have? What they'd just experienced was insane. Impossible. She'd never have believed it if she hadn't experienced it.

Just like she hadn't believed Riley.

Poor Riley. "Is she okay?"

Kimmie opened her mouth, but instead of saying something, she stared at April uncomfortably. April pushed her friend aside gently—

—and screamed when she saw the massive puddle of blood spreading out from a wound in Riley's neck and flowing around the drinking horn April had been holding when Riley passed out. There was blood inside it and a bloody lip print, as if someone had been sipping from the horn.

And next to it, being slowly obscured by blood, a Tarot card. King of Pentacles.

"Who did this?" she asked.

"You did," said Jenny.

April looked up and saw everyone there staring at her with the same horrible expression that Kimmie's face seemed frozen in.

Not one of them argued with Jenny.

"Bullshit." April turned back to Kimmie. "I would never."

Kimmie shook her head. "Sheila made you."

"How many times do I have to tell you, Ouija boards aren't—"

"I saw her," Kimmie said. "I'm sorry, April, it's true."

Then April saw it — Jenny had turned Kimmie against her.

"Spencer, you believe me," she tried.

But he wouldn't look at her.

"Look at your hand," Kimmie said.

April did. Somehow she'd burned it — but in the shape of the symbol that Jenny had drawn on her?

"Sheila can possess us," Kimmie explained. "The mark gets branded on our skin when she does."

April opened her mouth to ask, but Kimmie added: "We don't know why."

"Sheila wanted seven sacrifices, and four have died," Noah said. "What happens if she gets all seven?"

"Then she gets her revenge," Jenny said.

"Murders my grandmother, you mean." Why was anyone listening to this bitch?

After a long, uncomfortable silence, April switched gears. "Okay, so where are all these extra rooms coming from?"

"Maybe we're being teleported somewhere else?" Kimmie suggested.

"It's obvious." Toby held up his Rubik's cube. "This is the house." He twisted the top row of the cube. "Voila, a new configuration. Every time the ghost wants to attack, she moves things around."

"But how?" April asked, trying to keep the whine from her voice.

Toby shrugged. "Maybe the rules of physics are different for ghosts."

"Or maybe it's a hallucination," Spencer jumped in. "Because that would be the logical explanation."

"Our room was Tarot-themed. King of Pentacles." Jenny gave April an expectant look. Expecting her to know — what?

Oh. "That was the card I drew for Riley."

"And?"

Oh no. "Now Riley is dead."

April's head whirled as she recalled the cards she'd pulled earlier. She had been doing relationship readings — not predicting their deaths.

And she'd drawn the Death card for herself.

Panic gnawed on her insides, making it hard to breathe, move, or think.

Kimmie produced the Tarot deck she'd taken from Sheila's office and held it up. "We should burn it."

Noah bit his lip, then walked to the far corner of the attic, where they'd put Zach's corpse. After a moment's hesitation, he knelt by the body, shoved his hands in the pants pockets, one after another, and retrieved a lighter from the second one.

"Sorry, buddy," Noah whispered.

Noah tossed the lighter to Kimmie, who caught it and held it up to one end of the deck.

Flick.

Flick.

Flick.

The spark caught. Kimmie let the flame lick at the edge of the deck, running it along the short side of the cards.

But they wouldn't catch.

"Why isn't it working?" she asked.

"Maybe you still need them," Jenny said.

"Or maybe they're cursed," April added, turning to Kimmie. "After you made the water wheel appear, you imagined the door was unlocked, and it opened. Maybe you can make the doors open now."

Jenny snorted. "Unlikely."

"What will it hurt to try?" April asked.

"Nothing," Kimmie said.

April clapped. "Downstairs, people."

Minutes later, Kimmie stared at the front door, with everyone clustered behind her.

She screwed her eyes shut for a moment, then she reached for the doorknob and twisted.

But it didn't open.

"Why doesn't it work?" April asked.

"Because this house is real," Jenny said. "There's no psychic energy for Kimmie to manipulate here."

"Then how is the ghost keeping us from leaving?"

Jenny shrugged. "Want to get the Ouija board and ask her?"

"So, what?" April asked. "We just sit here and wait to die?"

No one replied.

Fine, she would have to figure it out.

April turned toward the stairs and caught sight of the open door to Sheila's office. "What about all the books in there? Maybe the answer's in one of them?"

"Great idea." Kimmie smiled, and April felt the tightness around her heart loosen a little. "Everybody grab an armful."

But as April exited the office with her pile of books, she couldn't help but notice how Kimmie hung back with Jenny, waiting for the others to head upstairs.

Because she wanted to make sure that everyone stayed together?

Or because she wanted to talk to Jenny without anyone overhearing?

April wouldn't rest until she found out.

✦

Kimmie sighed and put down the book she'd been flipping through. The same kind of book that April used to obsess over, all about meditating with crystals and directing your prana, and visualizing your chakras. Nothing was in it about ghosts, shapeshifting houses, or murder by possession.

It wasn't the kind of book a real psychic would read to learn from — it was the kind of book they'd sell to a client who wished they had psychic powers.

She took out Sheila's cursed deck and riffled through the cards again.

She counted them and now had only seventy-four. Four sacrifices, four missing cards.

She counted again, to be sure.

Seventy-four.

The floorboards creaked. Kimmie looked up and saw Toby looming over her.

"Can I talk to you?"

She wanted to say no, but what could he do while everyone else watched? All she had to do was yell for help, and both Spencer and Noah would come running. April, too — she never failed to put herself between Kimmie and Toby's creeping.

"Sure," she sighed. "What's up?"

"Have you thought about what I said before? About Spencer?"

"Enough of that," Kimmie said.

"He murdered Quinn," Toby said softly like he was murmuring sweet nothings to her instead of slinging accusations. "Noah might have helped; they were both right next to the body when I got there."

"No way, neither of them would—"

"I'm concerned for your safety, Kimmie." And he seemed so sincere; she didn't doubt it.

But— "If they did anything, it wasn't them; It was Sheila."

He scoffed. "You're smarter than that."

"I saw her," Kimmie insisted. "She drank Riley's blood. She winked at me."

"I saw too. I saw my own sister stab one of her best friends in the neck." Toby's jaw muscles pulsed. "I'm trying to help you stay alive."

"Well, I wish you would help us all stay alive."

She grabbed another book from the pile and pretended to read it.

Toby took it from her hand, turned it right side up, and gave it back to her.

"I hope you find what you're looking for," he said before leaving.

Why did she feel he wasn't talking about the book?

◆

April felt dead inside. Except she wasn't dead, she was alive, and four of her friends were dead.

And she couldn't explain how. Or why.

I did not kill Riley. I would never kill Riley.

Why would Kimmie accuse her of such a terrible thing?

And how could the others back her up?

She wanted to blame it on the weed — some sort of bad trip where she hallucinated her friends turning on her. But the happy, floaty feeling had worn off hours ago. And if Zach had more, he hadn't offered it to anyone.

She refused to believe that she'd killed Riley. Just like she refused to think that Riley would kill Zach. Or that Quinn would kill Brittany. Or that Spencer would kill Quinn.

It was insane.

But the worst part was Kimmie. Accusing April, then "forgiving" her because the "ghost" had made her do it?

It was so obvious that Goth Barbie had done it. Jenny wasn't part of the group. They had no idea who she was or where she came from. She'd probably manipulated Toby into asking her to prom.

Yet Kimmie kept looking to Jenny for answers instead of believing April, her best friend since fifth grade.

She didn't know how Jenny had tricked Kimmie into thinking she'd seen a ghost, but she was going to figure it out.

Maybe she had a costume stashed somewhere in the house?

Or some hidden projector?

Could she have hypnotized Kimmie?

Or given her a drug that would make her think she saw a ghost?

No, she would've had to fool everyone. Because everyone else had said the same thing.

It made more sense that there was a ghost.

Or that there was someone else in the house.

But that seemed even more unlikely. If they couldn't get out, how could someone else get in?

No, it had to be Jenny.

April was going to prove it.

Then she was going to make Jenny pay.

◆

When Noah came over and sat beside her, Kimmie was on her fifth book. "How are you doing?"

"Pretty much how you'd think." At least he smiled a little. "You?"

"Same."

Kimmie put the book down and watched the others — the friends she had left. Spencer sat with his arm around April, trying to coax her into a better mood. Jenny sat crossed-legged on a box, hands resting on her knees, eyes closed. Meditating?

And Toby, playing with that fucking Rubik's cube, unfazed by the death that surrounded him.

Kimmie experimented with leaning against Noah ever so slightly.

He responded by putting his arm around her waist and leaning toward her. It was kind of nice. Comforting. A happy place.

"You don't happen to have a plan, do you?"

"No," he said, "but there has to be a logical explanation for what's happening."

"Which is?"

"I don't know yet."

"You're not buying the haunted house explanation?"

He pulled back to look down at her, suddenly serious. "The important thing is when we finally get out of here, will anyone else buy the haunted house explanation?"

"What do you mean?"

"If the sheriff comes by to check on us tomorrow, which he will, when our parents realize we never came home, he will find four bodies and six suspects. What story do you think he's going to believe?"

She hadn't thought that far ahead. Oh my god, they were all going to jail.

"But what else can we tell them?" She asked. "That a serial killer dropped by our after-prom party to celebrate with us?"

"I think we ought to coordinate with Spencer and April. If we all say the same thing and make it easy for the sheriff to decide who did it …"

Kimmie was having a hard time believing what she was hearing. "Are you saying we blame Jenny and Toby?"

"I'm saying we cover our asses and make sure our stories agree."

"As far as we know, Jenny and Toby haven't done anything." She picked at the cover of the book in her lap. "I can't lie about that."

Noah nodded before answering. "Think about it. It's all our futures at stake, not just yours."

But it was Jenny's future at stake too. And Toby's.

Could she ruin theirs to save herself?

◆

Noah leaned back against the attic wall, struggling to keep his breathing slow and even. He was in worse shape than the last time he'd had a concussion, maybe the worst condition he'd ever been in his life. Or maybe it just felt that way because he couldn't go to the hospital and get pumped full of painkillers and anti-nausea drugs. He would've given just about anything to lie perfectly still in a soft bed in an air-conditioned room and stare at the ceiling until the doctors permitted him to sleep.

But he doubted he was going to make it to the hospital. Even if he wasn't attacked by one of his friends — or the ghost, depending on who you believed — he doubted he could stay awake until sunrise.

And once he fell asleep, he'd die.

So he would sit here and watch his friends for as long as he could keep his eyes open. The last thing he saw was going to be the people he cared about.

He wished he could say goodbye to his parents, who'd sacrificed so much to support his desire to play football. Dad had worked extra nights and weekends to pay for training camps and a private coach during the off-season. Mom had researched every piece of gear, and determined that he would have the best equipment they could afford. And they'd both come to every practice and game they could, cheering themselves hoarse so he'd know they were in the bleachers, rooting for him.

He wished he'd had a chance to finish with Kimmie. He'd loved seeing her surprised pleasure when he'd touched her and wanted her to be his first. There was a necklace in his duffel that he'd planned to give her afterward to show her how much he liked her. But even if they survived this, it was clear that he wouldn't be getting the girl. When Kimmie had been terrified, she hadn't looked to Noah — she'd looked to April.

April was as clueless about Kimmie's affection as Noah had been about Spencer's, which was another thing he would die wishing he could change. He wondered what he could've done differently to make Spencer trust him. Not that he was attracted to his best friend, but he wished he could've been there for him. Maybe if Spencer had been able to tell his secret sooner, he could've moved on from Noah, found another guy at school he could love. But instead, he'd spent what might be his last night alive angry at everyone who supposedly cared about him.

Noah wondered how much of Spencer's pent-up anger was Noah's fault for not being open to the truth.

And poor Toby had taken the brunt of that anger.

He couldn't change any of it.

So Noah stayed still. He breathed carefully, and prayed he'd get another chance to make things right.

THE LOVERS

TWENTY-THREE

The pain in April's head was making it hard to see. She knew they were all in the crazy, demonic attic of a haunted house of horrors, but the feeble light of the camping lantern and candles made it feel like they were in a bubble of light floating in the darkness of space.

She wished she were in a bubble in space. She wished she was anywhere else but here. April peered at the three people who shared her bubble.

Noah, who could barely walk without puking.

Jenny looked like a fierce goth doll but might be all show.

And Kimmie, who had hidden behind April all through sixth grade, when Cheryl and a couple of other bullies from the volleyball team decided that Kimmie was their next target. April remembered sticking up for Kimmie and how she had left a scratch on Cheryl's cheek that took more than a month to heal.

None were up to the challenge of fighting off an attack from Spencer, even in his exhausted state. They would be in trouble even if Cheryl and her friends showed up looking for revenge.

She sighed and walked over to the boxes that the others had been tearing through, surveying the piles of junk they'd been sorting onto the floor. She looked in a box containing a pile of papers, old letters by the look of them, and saw a glint of metal.

She reached in and took out a letter opener. She held it in front of her with both hands, like a two-handed sword, and lifted it up, for a moment losing herself in the fantasy that she was a kick-ass warrior queen.

Sighing as the vision faded, she stuck it into her back pocket and looked over to see that Kimmie was sitting on the top step of the stairs. She hauled herself up and went over to plunk herself down dramatically next to her.

Kimmie looked up quickly, barely acknowledging her with a blank stare, and then looked back down again. April wished Kimmie would say something. April hadn't felt this lonely since—

—since before she'd met Kimmie. She had felt a close connection to the nervous, dark-haired girl assigned the seat next to her. Within just an hour, Ms. Massey had to call them out for passing notes, and by the end of the day, they'd braided each other's hair and "painted" each other's nails with markers. Fairies and flowers, stars and rainbows.

April had thought it was her psychic powers that made her connection to Kimmie possible. She'd been disappointed when Kimmie wanted to stop practicing the visualizations with her, consoling herself with the thought that she could use her gift for both of them.

Except ... all of that had been a lie. A lie that Kimmie, who did have powers after all, had allowed April to believe.

For years.

Betrayal was the hardest thing to swallow. April had always known that she could be fooling herself about being psychic. But her faith in Kimmie's friendship had been unshakeable. The only stable thing in her universe.

"When did you know?" she asked Kimmie.

Kimmie stirred herself from her thoughts. "Know what?"

"That you were psychic. And I'm not." April tried to keep her voice light, but even she could hear the bitterness.

Kimmie sighed. "Before I met you, I had dreams that came true. Not all of them, but the ones that did were usually of bad stuff. I thought I was making those things happen."

"You never told me that."

"My mom took me to a psychiatrist because I was afraid to fall asleep," Kimmie continued. "I had to take these pills that made everything feel far away and wavery. Like I was underwater all the time. So I lied. I said the dreams had gone away. POOF! All better."

Anger warred with sympathy in April's heart. "You could've told me. I would've believed you."

Kimmie just shrugged, like it didn't matter whether April would've believed her or not.

"So, did the dreams go away?"

"I just got used to them."

"Then why wouldn't you want to develop the powers you already had?"

Kimmie hesitated for a moment. Had she ever talked about this with anyone?

"When we were doing all those meditation exercises together, I started seeing things." Kimmie's voice cracked under the pressure of her confession. "I thought I was going crazy. That my Mom would send me to a psych ward, that they would give me something stronger than those pills, and I would never escape from it all."

Poor Kimmie. April put her arm around her best friend and hugged her closer. "I'm so sorry. If I'd known, I wouldn't have pressured you to keep doing them."

Kimmie wiped her face on the back of her hand, leaving flecks of dried blood stuck to her tear-streaked cheek.

"It was the same thing, but worse, seeing bad things that were going to happen. Except now it was happening when I was awake."

"What kinds of things did you see?" April asked.

"My mom getting fired, two jobs ago. All of your breakups. The time I got my period in the middle of the spelling bee." Kimmie laughed. "It was nice to get a heads-up on that one."

April smiled. "Are the visions always bad?"

For some reason, that made Kimmie blush harder than April had ever seen her redden before.

"There's one I've had for years that I wish would come true."

"Only one?" April squeezed Kimmie tighter. "What happens in it?"

"This," Kimmie said.

Then she leaned over and kissed April.

For a moment, April forgot how to breathe. She felt hollow, floaty, and somehow more solid than she'd ever been. More real.

It had never been like this with Spencer. Or any of the other boys she'd kissed.

Kimmie pulled away, shy all of a sudden.

"You should've done that a long time ago," April said.

A noise came from below, down the staircase.

Spencer emerged into the dim light, his face torn, lurching up the stairs.

Kimmie and April scrambled to get out of the way just in time for Spencer to collapse on the floor right where they had been sitting.

He was holding his throat with one hand, trying to lift himself with the other.

Surging with adrenaline, April helped Kimmie quickly roll him over and saw the blood squirting between his fingers. "Toby …"

Toby. At the mention of her brother, April reflexively tuned in, and listened for where he was. Listened for the incessant click, click, click of his Rubik's cube.

But the sound had stopped.

THE CHARIOT

TWENTY-FOUR

Kimmie and April looked at one another, and without saying a word, both headed down the stairs with Kimmie in the lead. April grabbed the camping lantern and followed, which elicited surprised complaints from the others they were leaving behind.

They found a blood covered Toby on the ground floor, in the living room, surrounded by beer bottles, soda cans, and snack bags. The Rubik's cube was lying next to him, broken. One of its corner cubes was snapped off and lying a few inches away from it among the party trash.

April pushed past Kimmie, thrusting the lantern into her hands. She grabbed two handfuls of his shirt and yanked him upward. He seemed completely out of it, and she shook him until his eyes popped open. "What did you do?"

"What happened? We were getting food, and—"

Toby held his bloody hands up to ward her off. He saw them, and his eyes frogged out. He started hyperventilating. "Oh shit, is everyone okay?"

"You killed Spencer!"

April shook Toby so hard that his head wobbled like a bobblehead. Then she threw him back down again, hard.

Kimmie winced when his head hit the floor with a loud crack.

There was only anger now.

"Ow! What the hell!" Toby clutched his head as he rolled onto his side and tried to crawl away from April.

Kimmie lunged, trying to catch April's arm, but missed.

April followed Toby, kicking his thigh, then his lower back, as he yelled, "I'm sorry! I'm sorry!"

She almost nailed him in the head before Jenny grabbed her from behind and restrained her.

"It's not his fault; it's Sheila," Jenny said. "Sheila killed Spencer."

But April was beyond reason. She tried in vain to free herself from Jenny's restraint. She threw her head back and screamed at the ceiling in inarticulate rage before sagging forward. Jenny almost lost her balance. Kimmie caught April's arm and got her shoulder under it. Between them, they carried April over to the couch and set her down, where she flopped forward, covering her face with her hands.

Toby cowered against an overstuffed chair, breathing hard. "I'm sorry! I don't remember anything!"

Noah wobbled, then sank onto the loveseat. He started breathing hard, and then the panting turned to dry heaves as he clutched his stomach. The sight of him sick like this filled Kimmie with terror.

Could you die of a concussion? What if it was more than that? What if he needed surgery? Or had irreparable brain damage? He might die tonight too, and it wouldn't even be death by ghost murder—just a plain old real-world head injury.

Caused by attempted ghost murder.

Kimmie couldn't stifle her laugh. It came out sounding suspiciously like a cackle.

This is it. I'm officially going crazy.

Jenny was the only one holding it together. "Everyone, take a deep breath. We're not going to beat Sheila by panicking."

"Beat Sheila." April stared dully at the coffee table, defeat in every line of her face.

Kimmie had never seen her like this. She did everything passionately — even in Kimmie's vision, where April's grandmother had beaten her for reading Tarot cards, she had sobbed passionately when it was done.

And she'd never given up, even though that beating was probably one of many. Instead, she persuaded Kimmie to keep the cards and books for her. She might even have convinced the librarian not to tell her mother that she'd kept checking those books out. Kimmie would bet that if April could find a job as a Tarot reader after graduation, she'd take it and keep that a secret from her mother too.

But this April was flaming out. And Kimmie didn't know if that spark would rekindled once it was gone.

Toby got shakily to his feet. "I'm sorry, whatever I did, I didn't mean to."

Noah started dry heaving again.

No, he was vomiting. All over his knees, his shoes, and the floor.

Kimmie watched the pale green liquid puddle around his once-shiny dress shoes. The buzzy voice murmured in the back of her head, but it was hard to determine what it was saying.

Not right, she finally understood it to say.

Of course, it wasn't. How could any of this be right?

Not right, the voice buzzed again. No card.

"April, which card did you draw for Spencer?"

"What difference does it make now?" April seemed utterly checked out.

Kimmie couldn't blame her. Kimmie would've loved to have one of those pills the psychiatrist used to give her right now.

"Which card?" Kimmie begged. "Please?"

"The Chariot." A bitter laugh. "Spencer was going to be highly successful … at dying."

Kimmie fanned out the cards of Sheila's deck. There it was, the Chariot.

She frowned and picked the Chariot out of the deck. She flicked it with her other finger. It was real.

After Zach had died, his Tarot card had appeared briefly next to his corpse, then disappeared from Sheila's deck. Same with Brittany's card. And Quinn's. And Riley's.

So, why did she still have Spencer's?

Kimmie shivered. Maybe the deck Kimmie held was some ghost deck she was hallucinating. Or a manifestation of Kimmie's guilt about the deaths of her friends. Maybe that's why the cards seemed to disappear.

She turned to Noah and held up the Chariot. "Do you see this card?"

He turned his head between dry heaves to squint at it. "Yes."

So much for that theory.

Could there be two identical decks in the house?

"Did you see one like this near Spencer when you passed him?"

"I wasn't looking …" Heave. Heave. Heave. "… but I don't think so."

Toby had attacked Spencer down here. If there was a second deck, maybe Sheila hadn't been able to get close enough to Kimmie's and had left a Chariot card from that deck down here.

Kimmie grabbed the lantern from the coffee table, then got down on her hands and knees, avoiding blood as she peeked under the overstuffed chairs and carved wooden coffee table. Nothing.

She checked under the loveseat. Nothing there either.

"What are you looking for?" asked Jenny.

Kimmie crawled around to the other side of the couch and peeked under.

The straight razor that Toby had found earlier. She reached under to grab it, forcing her fingers to close around the handle, sticky with Spencer's still-warm blood.

Gagging, she brought it out into the light and stared at it.

And she knew what the buzz had been trying to tell her.

The gun, the sword, the drinking horn — all of the earlier murder weapons — came from the house of Tarot that Sheila had been psychically projecting into their minds. And those weapons had all disappeared shortly after the attack.

Brittany had been the only exception. Quinn seemed to have strangled her, or suffocated her by shoving the thong down Brittany's throat. Kimmie didn't know which one had killed her.

But the straight razor continued to exist here in the real world.

She picked it up, jumped to her feet and stalked toward Toby. "This is what you used to kill Spencer, right?"

Toby looked uncertain, and suddenly she was sure he was faking all of it. His confusion. His regret.

"I–I guess so?" he said.

"Show me the backs of your hands," Kimmie demanded.

"What?" He'd gone from uncertain to wary in an instant. "Why?"

Kimmie flipped open the straight razor. "Do it."

Eyes wide with fear, he slowly stretched out his hands.

Just like Kimmie thought.

"No brand," she announced to the others. Then she turned back to Toby. "You weren't possessed. You killed Spencer on purpose."

"I did not. You can't prove that."

"You didn't?" Kimmie asked. "Or I can't prove it?"

He gaped at her.

"Because I can prove it."

Kimmie walked over to April and grabbed her wrist, holding it up in the air. "I saw Sheila possessing April, and this mark was on fire. Then Sheila left, and the mark was burned into April's skin."

She held up her other hand and ticked off the names with her fingers. "Riley shot Zach. Branded. Quinn strangled Brittany. Branded. Spencer stabbed Quinn. Branded." She shook April's hand for emphasis. "April … drinking-horned Riley. Branded. But you don't have a brand. Because you killed Spencer without Sheila's help."

The others stared at Toby, expressions of shock, horror, and outrage on their faces.

"You saw what a bully he was," Toby whined. "He never missed a chance to humiliate me."

"He said some mean things to you. And you slashed his face open."

A sudden calm seemed to wash over Toby. A sense of resolve.

He stood, straightening himself to his full height. "It was a matter of honor. Spencer was little more than an animal walking among us pretending to be a human being. He didn't know how to be a man. He didn't know how to treat women. Hence, he didn't deserve to live."

He turned to Kimmie, his tone suggesting that he expected her to understand. "I did it for you."

April let out a scream that writhed up from the depths after festering through years of pain, cracked and pieced itself back together, then broke as she lunged up from the couch at Toby.

Kimmie saw his face in moments that stretched out impossibly long, turning from smug into angry, then as April made contact with him, down into fear.

They were wrestling on the floor, landing punches, biting, scratching, and trying to hold each other down. It was like years of sibling fighting compressed and rolled into a single fight.

Everyone stood back, not knowing what to do. Toby had murdered Spencer, not because a ghost possessed him or because Spencer had bullied him, but for love. He'd made Spencer's death Kimmie's fault.

Toby was choking April. It looked serious; she pried at his thumbs with both hands to get some air. Desperately, April flailed about with her right hand, and it fell on a bottle, which she brought up and against his head. Kimmie was frozen in horror, struggling with whether this was really happening.

It shattered, sending Toby reeling away to escape the pain.

April got up to her knees, gasping heavily, recovering her breath while Toby put his hand to his head and drew it away, covered with blood. He looked mad. April looked at the trash covering the floor, the bottles, and then spied it: the Rubik's cube.

In one smooth motion, she scooped up the cube and lunged at Toby just as he started to stand. The cube connected with the side of his head, where the bottle had landed.

And then, again, and again.

April's arm smashed the Rubik's cube into Toby's face, his head, over and over, sharp, intense, targeted blows, driving him back.

Colorful pieces of plastic flew free in every direction. He threw his arms up to defend himself, backing away, but it wasn't enough.

He stepped on a bottle, sending him reeling backward headfirst into the stone mantlepiece of the fireplace. He dropped heavily to the ground, and April was on him in an instant, smashing him with the broken cube over and over until there was nothing left to hit him with.

She stood and hurled the last fragment, bouncing it off his bloodied, lifeless face.

She screamed in anguish again and collapsed.

Kimmie barely managed to catch her before her head hit the ground. She could've gotten hurt like Noah.

I could've lost them both.

A few minutes ago, Kimmie had been in heaven, staring into April's eyes and realizing that April had wanted that kiss. Maybe for as long as Kimmie had, even if she hadn't consciously realized it.

And now, this.

April would never be the same.

None of them would ever be the same, especially April.

How did you get over your brother killing your boyfriend — then avenging your boyfriend by killing your brother?

Were there enough psychiatrists in the world to fix April after something like this?

TWENTY-FIVE

Kimmie hugged April closer as she sobbed into the crook of Kimmie's neck.

Except for all the blood, the trauma, and the fact that they might die in the next few hours, the two of them could've been having a cozy snuggle on the threadbare loveseat.

April killed Toby.

Toby killed Spencer.

And neither of them could blame the ghost — both of them had killed of their own volition.

Kimmie couldn't imagine what that would be like. To kill your brother. How was April going to live with that?

She was a murderer.

Yes, Toby had been a creep. But Kimmie would never have guessed that he'd do something so evil.

And he'd blamed Kimmie for it.

Guilt twinged in her heart. If he hadn't been obsessed with me, would Toby still have killed Spencer?

Maybe. Spencer's constant dissing had been almost reflexive on his part, like an addiction he didn't even recognize. According to April, it had begun long before Kimmie's mom had brought her to Bellwether.

Kimmie hadn't done anything to encourage Toby's interest. Other than failing to let him know that she'd never date him before he'd decided to kill for her.

So she pushed away the guilt to focus on the present.

They were still trapped in the house.

Sheila only needed one more sacrifice to regain her power and return to the physical world.

And Noah still might die of a treatable concussion because they were trapped in a haunted house. He lay on the couch, occasionally moaning as he shifted positions, struggling to stay awake. Every time his breathing quieted, Kimmie stretched her leg out to poke his shoulder with her toe.

In the corner chair, Jenny pored over another of Sheila's books by the light of the camping lantern, looking for a banishing ritual. At least that's what she said she was doing. Kimmie wasn't sure if Jenny was genuinely sorry she'd summoned Sheila, not realizing what she was getting into, or if she still wanted to talk to the ghost. Her fear had seemed genuine, but could she be trusted to help them get out of this?

"Grandma used to make him watch," April said.

"Watch what?" Kimmie asked.

"Whenever she punished me." April raised her head and wiped her nose on the back of her arm. "So he would see what would happen if he wasn't a good boy."

"That's messed up," Jenny muttered without looking up from her book.

Like she should talk.

"I wasn't in love with Spencer," April continued, "but he didn't deserve to die like that."

"No one deserves to die like that." Kimmie grabbed April's hand and squeezed it.

Noah's eyelids closed. Kimmie gave him another poke, and he started, then rolled over onto his side and dry-heaved over the edge of the couch.

"Kimmie, when I die—"

"You're not going to die," Kimmie said. "We're going to stay together until someone finds us."

"My card was Death."

"Which means transformation, and you've told me that a million times." Kimmie squeezed April's hand again, taking comfort as much as giving it. She couldn't lose her, not after finally finding the courage to kiss her and being kissed back.

"But dying is a kind of transformation," April said, her voice quivering. "Transforming into a ghost. That's what happened to Sheila."

"Surviving is a kind of transformation, too," Kimmie countered. Surviving something as horrific as this.

Jenny snapped the book shut and reached for the next one on the pile.

"You haven't found anything yet?" Kimmie asked.

"Nothing specific," Jennie answered. "There are a lot of traditions that say ghosts can't manifest in sunlight or during the day, so it's possible that if Sheila doesn't get all seven sacrifices, she will go back to haunting this place until the next psychic comes along."

"Unless she's one of those ghosts that's fine with daylight," Kimmie said. "What about if she possesses someone? Will the sunlight drive her out?"

"I'm guessing not since she thinks taking over a body will help her get revenge."

"If we get out of here alive, I'm burning this place down." April slumped against Kimmie, laying a cheek against her shoulder. Heaven.

"So you're saying we can wait her out?" Kimmie asked.

"Or we could try to talk to her again through—"

"No," Kimmie and April said in unison.

"We could try to bargain with—"

"With what?" Kimmie huffed. "The only thing she wants is for us to die. All we can do is beg for our lives, and why would she back off when she's so close to getting what she wants?"

Noah finished dry heaving and rolled onto his back, panting.

Please stay awake until we can get out of here. Somehow it seemed worse that Noah might die of a concussion, something so normal and fixable if only he'd been able to get to a hospital. If Kimmie could save him, that would make tonight a little less terrible.

But that thought made her feel guilty — did she feel that way because she cared about him? Or did she want to save him to make up for the fact that, if they survived this, she would leave him for April?

"What happens if she gets the last sacrifice?" April asked.

"We don't even know if Toby's death counts or Spencer's," Jenny said. "Is it still a sacrifice if they died without Sheila's involvement?"

"Let's assume they do count," Kimmie countered. "What can Sheila do when she gets her full power?"

"Near as I can tell, she'll be able to manifest in the physical world."

"Manifest? Does that mean she assumes a physical form?"

Kimmie had been wondering that too. "Or would she return to her original body and become a zombie?"

April shuddered. "Zombies, that's the only thing that would make this nightmare worse."

"So far, the only powers we've seen her use are mental projections and possession," Jenny said. "So I'm guessing she needs a host."

"If she possesses one of us, how do we get her out?" Kimmie asked.

"I don't know. Kill the host, probably."

"Kill the host?" April looked like she wanted to kill Jenny. "You mean, kill one of us."

"What about the Tarot deck?" Kimmie asked. "Isn't there some way we can use it against her?"

"You're the only one here who has a connection to it. What do you think?"

The buzzy voice in her head was silent. "No idea."

Jenny pulled her feet up to the chair and hugged her knees. "Maybe we're coming at this from the wrong direction. What do we know about Sheila?"

"My grandmother hated her," April volunteered. "She's the reason I wasn't allowed to read about anything occult at home. She was always afraid Sheila would use her psychic powers to make Grandpa Warren come back to her."

"Did your grandmother ever say anything about Sheila's death?" Jenny asked.

"Good riddance."

Kimmie had to agree with Grandma Patricia on that one.

"So, I'm going to die tonight, and Sheila will go after my Grandma." April looked like she was about to start crying again.

"Maybe not." Jenny jumped to her feet. "Maybe we can create a banishing ritual."

Kimmie frowned. "Like a spell?"

"If you've known how to do that, why'd you wait?" April asked.

"Because real magic is tricky," Jenny said. "It made sense to see if we could find instructions on how to do it right before we started experimenting."

"What happens if we get it wrong?" Kimmie asked.

"Maybe nothing." Jenny shrugged. "Maybe Sheila kills us all. The only way to find out is to try."

Sometimes life doesn't give you a choice.

That's what Jenny had told Kimmie hours ago before this nightmare started.

Kimmie hated that she was right.

QUEEN OF SWORDS

TWENTY-SIX

K immie shuffled through the Tarot cards, looking for something that wasn't there. She'd been hoping the buzzy voice would tell her what to do, but it stayed silent.

She glanced at Noah, sitting cross-legged on the other side of the room as he stared at the floor. April sat across from him, talking to him, shaking him awake every time he started to nod off. He'd managed to stay awake, but could he make it to morning?

Jenny put her hand on Kimmie's shoulder. "We need to create a place of strength. Someplace that feels like your place instead of Sheila's."

"How do we do that?"

Jenny thought for a moment. "Pick a significator card. Something that represents who you are."

Kimmie riffled through the cards until she found the Queen of Swords, which April usually used to represent her in a reading. April said it was hers because swords were air signs, and Kimmie was a Gemini. But Kimmie had been drawn to the card anyway. She loved the cherubs on the throne and the determined expression on the woman's face. She looked like someone who knew what she wanted and went after it.

"Will this work?"

Jenny smiled, and Kimmie felt like she'd made the right choice.

"Now focus on the card, and zoom in closer, until you're inside the image."

Holding it in front of her, Kimmie imagined she was a bird flying toward the scene on the card, getting closer and closer until she almost slammed into it.

She felt a slight popping, buzzing feeling behind her eyes. Then her vision jumped, and her perspective shifted, snapping into place.

She was the queen, seated on the cherub throne, holding the sword in one hand while she raised the other toward the heavens. She could feel the weight of the crown encircling her head and the caress of silk against her skin.

She looked around her throne room, with its white marble floor shot through with veins of gold. The walls looked like … ivory? Bone? Something like that. The walls towered upward to a ring of carven cherubs circling the room, and above that, a dome-like ceiling arching high above them, filled with crystalline windows that scattered sparkling rainbows through the air.

Kimmie got up and backed away from her throne, setting the sword carefully on the floor before examining it. Ornately carved, made of the same material as the walls, the back shaped like sweeping butterfly wings, and the seat upholstered in white satin.

She reached up to remove her crown. It was silver, made of diamond-encrusted filigree butterflies, and three large opals glimmered in the front.

"You have to imagine us with you," said a distant voice.

She did, and suddenly there they were: Jenny, with her arms crossed around her midsection, nodding in appreciation. Noah was leaning against the wall, looking even sicker than before. April was next to him, her jaw dropping as she registered her new surroundings.

"It's beautiful," Kimmie breathed.

"You're the one who imagined it," said Jenny. "You're the last person in the world who should be amazed."

Then she got serious. "You need to believe this is real. If you start doubting, it will disappear, poof, and we'll be back in the house."

Shit. Just hearing that made her wonder, and the marble walls faded enough that Kimmie could see the faint outlines of the attic through their haze.

I'm the Queen of Swords, and this is my throne room.

The walls solidified again.

Jenny whipped out her Sharpie — from her cleavage? — and undid the long pink ribbon laced through her corset, then tied one end of the ribbon around the marker. "Okay, you keep doing whatever you're doing. I have an art project to get started on. Here, hold this end of the string on the floor."

Kimmie pressed her finger against the end of the string, holding it against the marble floor, while Jenny walked the other end with the Sharpie out to the full length of the ribbon and set the marker's tip to the white marble.

Kimmie remembered this from geometry class. She never thought she'd be putting it to practical use.

"Whatever you do, don't let go," she warned while drawing the circle with Kimmie's finger as the center.

"What happens if I let go?"

"We'll have to start over, dummy." Jenny went to work.

◆

While Jenny drew the magical circle for their ritual, Kimmie joined Noah, slumped against a wall and sipping a lukewarm ginger ale they'd grabbed from the overturned cooler. It seemed cruel to keep poking him awake when he would probably die tonight anyway. If she let him drift to sleep, he'd die peacefully.

But it wasn't her decision to make.

"My mom wanted me to be a doctor," he said so quietly that Kimmie almost missed it. "She's going to be so disappointed."

"Just a little longer, and you'll be at the hospital, getting better." She felt terrible promising it, when the odds of it happening were so low. But what else did you say to someone who might be dying? It was nice knowing you? She would rather have hope even if it was only a sliver.

"It would've been fun, Kimmie."

Where was this coming from?

"But if April's who you want, don't let her walk all over you," he added.

"Right now, I just want to get out of here." That was the truth, even if it wasn't the one he wanted to talk about.

Noah's head dipped closer, putting his lips right against her ear, tickling as he whispered. "Tell the sheriff it was Jenny's fault."

Then he lurched forward and threw up.

Kimmie didn't think he could make it through the ritual, let alone the night.

◆

April watched Kimmie as she comforted poor Noah. Just looking at him made her dizzy and sick to her stomach. The only thing keeping

April from having more hysterics was Kimmie, whose calm resolve made zero sense but somehow made April believe they would make it.

April touched her lips, remembering how it had felt to press them against Kimmie's. Before tonight, she'd never thought of Kimmie that way, but now she couldn't think of her any other way.

She thought about Kimmie's constant blushing — when they were changing clothes when she'd helped April pick out her bikini for the summer when they were doing something innocent, and April's hand brushed hers. All this time, she'd been so busy trying to date the right boy she'd been ignoring the person who loved her the most.

It had never occurred to April that she might be a lesbian. Or bisexual. Pansexual? Whatever. She'd been jealous of how close Quinn and Brittany had seemed, but she'd never been attracted to either of them. And she had been genuinely attracted to Spencer the other guys she'd dated. But maybe it wasn't about what you called yourself; maybe it was about how you loved the person you were with.

She loved Kimmie.

They'd wasted so much time they'd never get back. Even if they both survived, Kimmie would go to college, where she'd meet other girls who were much more intelligent than April. And even if Kimmie were willing to have a long-distance relationship, they'd only see each other on breaks and during the summer. It was too late for April to follow her, with her C average and lack of extracurriculars.

She'd gotten Kimmie just in time to lose her again.

Maybe it didn't matter. She'd drawn Death tonight, and so far, everyone's card had reflected how they died. Despite Kimmie's desperation to believe that the card predicted that April would undergo a transformation, April feared that Death meant actual death this time.

Maybe that was best for everyone.

Because Kimmie had kissed April but did she still have feelings for Noah? Before this evening imploded, Kimmie had planned to have sex with him. Maybe the kiss was part of the adrenaline rush, fooling

Kimmie into believing she loved April. Horror movies made you want to make out afterward, and they were trapped in a real-life horror movie, weren't they?

So when Kimmie came over to ask her how she was, she said, "You and Noah are so good together. If you want to stay with him when this is over—"

"No."

Kimmie's forcefulness made April's heart flutter. "

"I only want to be with you," Kimmie added.

"Even if I'm going to prison?" It was a bad joke, but April couldn't help herself.

"You won't. I'll swear that Toby tried to kill you and that it was self-defense. I'll make Jenny and Noah swear it too."

That was Kimmie, completely loyal. Except for tonight — which April understood, given how everything had happened — Kimmie had always stuck by her, no matter what.

"Maybe I deserve prison," April suggested. "Grandma Patricia says I'm a bad person."

"Toby was the evil one." Kimmie scowled. "And your grandmother is a home wrecker. Who cares what she thinks?"

April laughed. Even though she'd heard the stories, it was hard to imagine her mean old grandmother and her nearly-catatonic grandfather having a passionate affair behind the town psychic's back. She'd committed adultery, but Grandma punished April for reading Tarot books. Total hypocrisy.

"Whatever happens, I'm with you," April said. "We live, or we die; we do it together."

"Done." Jenny got up from the floor and put the cap back on her Sharpie. "Who wants to banish a ghost?"

THE MAGICIAN

TWENTY-SEVEN

Jenny and Kimmie sat across from one another with the Ouija board resting on their knees. Jenny had warned them to stay outside the ritual circle she'd drawn on the floor and embellished with a crazy assortment of curving, spidery symbols similar to those on her necklace.

Noah sat in the corner of the room, back to the wall, trying to stay upright. All three of them rested their fingertips on the planchette.

Standing guard. April stood between them and the circle, holding the sword like a baseball bat. Kimmie didn't know what good a sword would do against a ghost, but April insisted. And it was probably better for her to feel like she was doing something than to sit there and wait to die.

Jenny cleared her throat. "Restless spirit, we compel you to come to us. Pass through into the world of the living. Join us; we welcome you."

The planchette began to move, spelling out I ACCEPT in sweeping, eager motions.

But Kimmie's head didn't buzz like it had the first time they'd used the board. Not even a little bit. Did that mean Jenny was talking for Sheila?

Or had Kimmie used up all her power in projecting this room over the attic? Maybe she didn't have any psychic energy left over.

A blue, flickering glow began in the air, hanging in the circle's center. Sparkling rainbows that scattered throughout the room seemed to shy away from it as it took form. Floating in the air, a beautiful woman, wreathed in blue flame emerged from the darkness..

Sheila settled on the marble floor.

She turned and smiled, walking towards them.

April raised the sword high, grunting with the effort as Kimmie jumped to her feet and stepped backward. Jenny, who'd been balancing the Ouija board on her knees, set it aside, then stood up as If waiting to greet Sheila.

Sheila responded by moving faster, still smiling sweetly. She leapt forward and splashed against an invisible wall like a bucket of glowing water thrown against a big glass window. Prismatic flames sprung up all around the perimeter of the circle.

Holy crap, it worked.

Jenny looked triumphant.

April held her ground, adjusting her grip on the sword's hilt.

Kimmie wasn't sure if she should join them or stay where she was.

On the one hand, if she lost focus, this space would disappear, and maybe the ritual circle would vanish too.

On the other hand, April looked scared, and Jenny — Kimmie had no idea if she knew how to banish the ghost now that they'd caught her. What if Sheila escaped and possessed her?

April might panic. It might be up to Kimmie to kill Jenny.

Sheila coalesced from the spattered glow. Her eyes were completely black, and her features were skeletal. She looked furious.

"You can't hold me," rasped Sheila. "And when I escape, you'll be sorry."

"If you get out of there," Jenny replied.

"If you try to possess one of us, we're prepared to kill whoever it is," April added. "So don't even bother."

Sheila responded by erupting into a cloud of blue flame. Her voice rang out from the glowing plasma, "I will drown you all!"

Kimmie held her breath as water erupted from the center of the circle, but like Sheila, when it met the edge of the circle, it morphed into a rainbow of magical flames, then evaporated into nothingness. Sheila's scream filled the ivory room, cracking panes of glass high above them. Pieces of crystal rained on the marble floor like hail, making tinkling sounds around them.

The water gushed faster, roiling violently as it threw itself against the invisible barrier, but it couldn't break free of the circle.

It was working. Maybe they were going to survive this after all.

The water suddenly receded, and Sheila was back, a beautiful woman surrounded by ethereal flame. She focused her attention on Kimmie.

"Your talent is very strong, but you barely know how to use it. And you're tired. So tired, I can feel you weakening."

She was tired. She'd been up all night, fueled by terror, adrenaline, and grief as she watched her friends die. A second's slip in her focus, and the ghost might escape. Taking her, or worse, taking April from her.

Despair crept through Kimmie as Sheila continued, a seeping darkness that sapped all her strength. The walls of her throne room turned a little less opaque.

Why didn't Jenny do something?

"Give up, and I'll let you live." Sheila bared her teeth — or maybe that was supposed to be a smile. "I'll even spare one of your friends. You can choose which."

Sheila flamed brighter and began to grow until she filled the entire circle from floor to ceiling. She raised her hands, palms forward, and placed them on the invisible barrier.

The barrier began to glow, edging toward incandescent. Kimmie could feel Sheila pushing against the circle. Against Kimmie's mind.

"Jenny, start the banishing," Kimmie said through gritted teeth. She willed the walls back into existence. Sheila stood before Kimmie's throne. Kimmie was the queen here.

April, still standing guard, wielded Kimmie's sword.

"Or, if you'd like, I can teach you to use your power. Before I died, I had a connection beyond the veil, but what have I learned since?" Sheila chuckled. "I can make you immortal. You could be a queen in the real world. All you have to do is set me free."

"She doesn't want to be immortal!" April snarled. "She's never wanted to be psychic."

"Because she doesn't appreciate the talent she's been given," Sheila replied. "But you do, don't you?"

"Jenny, now!" Kimmie had never focused this long or this intensely on anything. Not even when she'd been practicing visualizations with April.

The walls grew transparent again, thin enough that Kimmie could make out one of the attic windows.

She was losing.

She thought about Zach, the moment before he'd died, clutching the bleeding gunshot wound in his stomach.

Quinn sliced open by a sword that had disappeared.

Brittany with bruises around her neck, and her thong stuffed down her throat.

Riley with blood bubbling on her lips as she died.

Spencer's face sliced so deeply that bone shone through the cuts, and Toby with his head bashed in.

Fury filled her. She would not let this monster escape back into her world. She would die first.

The room brightened around her, more solid than ever before.

"The whole point of a summoning circle is to make a pact with the entity you've summoned," Sheila smirked, seeming confident as ever despite Kimmie's new strength. "This is your chance to change your life forever. Everything you've ever wanted is possible."

"I. Want. My. Friends. Back."

Sheila's form bubbled as if she was about to boil.

She turned toward April. "You, on the other hand, have nothing to bargain with. You have no gift. If you want to live, your only choice is to convince Kimmie to make a deal with me."

"Why would I do that when Kimmie's beating your ass?"

April's arms had to be tired, but she brandished the sword, aiming the tip at Sheila's face.

"Your grandmother drowned me to keep your Warren from leaving her. She found out he was planning to come back to me."

"Liar!" But April's arms started to quiver.

"I've been planning my revenge for years," Sheila said. "And I'll start by punishing you. Make her watch you suffer. Only Kimmie can save you."

The tip of the sword wavered as April glanced at Kimmie.

Kimmie tried to ignore the fear in her eyes. The only way to save April was to make sure Sheila couldn't return. "Jenny!"

But Jenny seemed entranced as Sheila turned that terrible smile on her.

"I haven't forgotten about you, little Jenny." Sheila stared piercingly at Jenny, forcing her to take a step back. "You were braver than the rest of them put together."

"That's enough," said Kimmie.

She raised one hand and imagined the Queen of Swords appearing in it — and it did, its edges glowing incandescent. The only difference between this card and Sheila's deck is that the woman on the throne wore Kimmie's face.

She recited the words they'd chosen earlier:

"Sheila, I command you to leave this world. You are hereby banished to the afterlife forever."

But the symbols around the ritual circle didn't light up like Jenny had said they should.

The crushing pressure around Kimmie's mind remained.

Sheila's mocking laugh shook the room. "A priest couldn't exorcize me, but you thought you could do the job? Pathetic. Warren spent plenty of money trying to get rid of me, but I bound my soul to this house when I was still alive. I knew that whore Patricia would try to kill me."

Sheila made a gesture, and the card in Kimmie's hand burst into flame.

Kimmie dropped it before it burned her fingers, but dark despair returned as she saw herself turning to ash.

She was failing.

THE HIGH PRIESTESS

TWENTY-EIGHT

"**W**ait!" Jenny's voice came from behind Kimmie.

Kimmie turned to see Noah lying face down and Jenny straddling him, lifting his head by his hair with one hand and holding a knife to his neck.

The dagger from Kimmie's dream. Where had she conjured it from?

"What are you doing?" Kimmie took a step closer, but Jenny moved the knife a tiny bit, and a line of blood appeared on Noah's neck.

"You made me kill her," Jenny said to Sheila.

Drowning in the staircase. Waking up to Maisie stalking her. Grabbing the dagger from the altar and stabbing Maisie in the neck.

"You were the catatonic sister," Kimmie said. "You killed Maisie."

"She made me kill Maisie! Sheila possessed her and made her try to kill me. Just like April killed Riley."

April made a choked sound behind Kimmie.

But Kimmie didn't dare take her eyes off Jenny, not with that blade at Noah's throat.

"If she can come back, she can tell me how to bring Maisie back," Jenny continued.

"You don't know that," Kimmie replied.

"What do you think I've been doing for the last eight years, studying for my SATs?" Jenny turned back to Sheila. "Bring Maisie back, and I'll give you the seventh sacrifice."

"Jenny, no!"

Kimmie wasn't close enough to try to grab the knife away, and she wasn't sure she could do it without hurting Noah anyway.

"If you let her out, she won't keep her word. She'll kill all of us just because she can."

"Shut up; I'm not talking to you." Jenny gazed up at Sheila. "Give Maisie back, and you can do whatever you want. I don't care."

Sheila laughed, and the flames fluttered and swayed around her as she stood at the center of a dust devil. Or a vortex of evil.

"Maisie had the gift." The buzz in Kimmie's head rose and fell with the rhythm of Sheila's words, like a staticky echo. She was losing control.

Sheila continued: "But Maisie wasn't trained. She didn't have the skill to anchor her soul to this place when you killed her."

Kimmie's will was failing under the constant pressure of Sheila's. She was so tired. But the second she failed, she and April would be dead.

So she turned to Jenny. "Maisie is gone. But you can keep Sheila from killing anyone else."

"I killed Maisie. She won't forgive me until I bring her back." Jenny's eyes got a bit wilder, and Kimmie realized she'd said the wrong thing.

"Sheila said Maisie is gone. Like totally gone. Would your sister want you to kill Noah for nothing?"

"She'd want her life back."

Think, Kimmie. "What's the point of bringing Maisie back if you never see her again?"

"Why wouldn't I—"

"Even if you survive, you won't get away with killing seven people."

"I only killed Noah." Jenny was sweating, and her hands were shaking. Kimmie prayed that Jenny wouldn't accidentally cut Noah's throat before Kimmie could think of a way to dissuade her. "Besides, do you think they will believe your story about a ghost possessing your friends and turning them into murderers? They put me in a psych ward for saying nothing."

Kimmie's worst nightmare — spending the rest of her life drugged up and staring at the walls like a zombie, knowing that no one believed her, that nothing she could say would break her free.

Knowing she would never see April again.

"They won't have to believe me," Kimmie said. "Everyone saw you with Toby at prom. Everyone knows you went with us afterward."

Jenny looked from Kimmie to Sheila.

Sheila smiled a predator's smile. "There might be a way to bring Maisie back, but you'll have to help me first. Kill the boy, and together, we'll avenge your sister."

The buzzing in Kimmie's head was so intense that it almost blotted out Sheila's voice altogether. But she couldn't make out what it was trying to tell her.

"And after you kill the boy, kill the granddaughter of the woman who murdered me," Sheila added.

"How!" Kimmie yelled, stalling for time. "Make her tell you how she will bring Maisie back!"

Jenny looked at Sheila. "How?"

"Once I'm anchored in the physical realm, I can bring you through the veil so that you can search for her soul. It's possible she could be bound to you."

"Maisie would live in my head?" Jenny asked.

"Until you found a body for her." Sheila leered at April. "She'd probably do."

Shit. What was left to do other than an appeal to Jenny's better nature? She conjured another card from Sheila's deck. The High Priestess.

"This is who you said you are, Jenny. You said it yourself. You're the keeper of wisdom. Revealer of hidden things. Not a murderer."

"I'm also a murderer. Haven't you been listening?"

"Sheila killed Maisie by possessing her."

Jenny sniffed back tears. "If I hadn't snuck in to see the seance, she'd still be alive."

"There was no way for you to know what would happen. You killed Maisie in self-defense."

"I should've been the one to die."

Jenny plunged the knife into Noah's neck and dragged it toward her. Noah's strangled scream quickly became a gurgle as his body spasmed and blood spurted over the floor.

The barrier around Sheila glowed white-hot. Then it flickered out.

Sheila's laugh shook the room. She made a gesture with her hand, and the Tower card appeared. A tall, dark brick building with people falling out as lightning ripped it apart, dislodging its crown-like roof.

The buzzing in Kimmie's head swarmed through her as a tornado of light exploded outward from the ghost, blinding her.

The house creaked and moaned as the tornado of light tore through it, and Kimmie curled into a ball, trying to make herself tiny. Wood groaned, and metal shrieked as the magical storm clawed the house apart.

Debris flew through the air — boards, drywall, insulation — and Kimmie tried to cover her head with her hands as the hail of destruction battered her. She could hear things crashing into the walls around her, smashing furniture and shattering glass.

Kimmie staggered backward, tripped over something, and landed hard on her tailbone.

She dropped the High Priestess, but it no longer mattered. Sheila was free and had the power of seven deaths to fuel her.

Something brushed Kimmie's ankle. Splinters pierced the flesh of her fingers, leaving them hot and slippery. She screamed and kicked at whatever it was, then launched herself to all fours, hands scrabbling against the rotting wood floors as she tried to crawl away.

The floor tilted, and she was hurled against the wall.

The impact knocked the breath out of her, and she lay gasping for air, trying to make sense of what was happening.

There was a final deafening crash, then the light dissipated as quickly as it had appeared, and Kimmie blinked until tears cleared the dust from her eyes.

When her vision finally cleared, she saw that Noah's body lay still on the floor in a pool of his blood on the parlor floor. And beyond him, a huge hole was torn in the wall. Through it, she could see the glow of the coming sunrise, pinking the horizon.

There are a lot of traditions that say ghosts can't manifest in sunlight …

Kimmie's head swam in the silent aftermath of the destruction. Jenny had killed Noah right in front of her. And if what Jenny had said was true, Sheila would have the strength to claim a living body now.

She didn't dare believe that the sunrise had come in time. She had to assume that Sheila had won.

Kimmie was still herself. Which meant Sheila had to be in—

THE TOWER

TWENTY-NINE

Jenny crawled out from behind the overturned couch, now partially buried in a pile of small debris: wedges of rotting drywall from the walls and ceiling, chunks of two-by-fours from within the walls that the vortex of power had torn apart.

April huddled under the coffee table, which had stopped a falling ceiling beam from crushing her. Her breath came in jagged sobs as she squirmed from under it and crawled toward Kimmie.

"Stop," Kimmie croaked.

But April kept coming, so Kimmie lunged for the dagger that Jenny had dropped. As soon as her fingers closed over the hilt, she forced herself to her feet. She held the dagger in front of her like she'd seen people do in movies. "I mean it, stay there."

"What are you doing, Kimmie?" April whined. "Help me."

Jenny was the one who'd killed Noah to bargain with Sheila for Maisie's return. So it should be Jenny whose body Sheila would choose to possess.

Except … Sheila wanted to kill Patricia, who'd drowned her, to keep her from stealing April's grandfather Warren back.

Wouldn't that be easier to do if she'd chosen to possess April's body?

Kimmie swallowed hard and tightened her grip on the dagger. Could she do this? Could she kill April, who she'd loved since fifth grade?

"I have to know if you're you," Kimmie said.

"Who else would I be?"

April's confusion was almost comical. Lost puppy dog adorable. But behind it, there was a blankness that terrified Kimmie. She'd been through hell. They all had. She was probably in shock. Of course, she wouldn't act like her usual self.

But if she didn't act like herself, how could Kimmie tell if Sheila was controlling her?

"That's not April," Jenny said.

"Or you're not Jenny," Kimmie countered. "Prove that you are."

"When we were downstairs alone you asked me a question before all this started. What was it?"

"I asked you why you were into all this goth shit."

"No, you asked me, why not be normal?"

Kimmie nodded. Those had been her exact words.

Jenny continued: "What did I tell you?"

"You said sometimes life doesn't give you a choice." But— "That doesn't prove anything. Sheila could've overheard us talking, couldn't she?"

"Okay, fine. Something that happened at prom."

"How do we know that Sheila can't read our thoughts while possessing us?"

"I don't know what to tell you," Jenny said. "We just met tonight. You know her" pointing to April. "much better."

April shifted onto her knees and raised her hands toward Kimmie, palms up like a toddler begging to be picked up.

"Please, Kimmie, I want to go home."

"Is that how she normally acts?" Jenny asked.

"She's in shock." I'm probably in shock too. None of this felt real except for the buzzing in her head and the textured metal grip of the dagger against her palm. There was no way to be sure.

"I'm not Sheila. I'm me," Jenny continued in a calm voice. "Killing me won't keep you safe."

"I'm me too," April added quickly, fear dawning on her face. "I'm me, Kimmie. I-I love you."

But that didn't prove anything either. Unless it was Sheila trying to manipulate Kimmie.

She couldn't use the protection symbols to tell. April already had the brand from when Sheila had possessed her earlier. Jenny's hand still bore the symbol in marker, but maybe it only got burned into a person's flesh when Sheila left their body.

If she was still in there, the mark might remain unchanged.

"How do I know you're not Sheila, and killing April is the first part of your revenge?"

"I'm disappointed that she didn't take me." Jenny took a step forward and held out her hand. "I'll make Sheila jump from April to me. Then we'll disappear, and you can have April back."

"I thought the only way to get rid of Sheila was to kill the host," said Kimmie.

"I'll find another way. I'll ask my coven for help."

Scuffing sounds behind Kimmie. Is April getting to her feet, maybe? Kimmie was afraid to look away from Jenny. "Are you okay, April?"

"Yeah," April quavered. "Is Noah dead?"

Kimmie nodded.

Jenny took another sideways step and smiled bitterly. "Give me Sheila, and you can blame the deaths on me."

When Kimmie said nothing, she added, "You know that's going to happen, right? Everyone's going to blame you because you survived. If you're lucky, they'll decide you're too traumatized to be held responsible and put you in a psych ward."

How much longer could Kimmie stall? Someone had to have seen the house explode. Someone had to be on their way.

A bottle hurtled past Kimmie's shoulder and slammed into Jenny's, shattering into pieces and sending shards of glass flying everywhere.

Jenny staggered back, lost her footing, and toppled with a shriek.

Kimmie raised her arms to shield her face, but the glass cut her cheeks, chin, and wrists.

"What the—" Jenny clutched her shoulder. Dozens of tiny shards of glass peppered the side of her neck and her face, blood welling around each jagged piece. She pulled one out — dangerously close to her eye — and stared at it. "You bitch!"

April bolted through the opening in the wall, leaping over a pile of debris, then veering out of sight.

Kimmie ran after her, nearly tripping as the ragged hem of her dress caught on something, forcing her to yank hard to free herself. She slipped on the wet grass as the fabric tore, falling forward into a crouch, then scrambling back up to her feet. Behind her, Jenny cried out in pain.

Maybe she wouldn't follow. A face full of glass — that had to hurt a lot. And if she'd gotten a tiny piece in her eye... it would be agony.

April headed straight for the woods along the back of the house. Her apple red prom dress stark against the browns and greens forest, even in the dim light.

"April!" Kimmie shouted. "Don't stop!"

But Kimmie hesitated, not sure if she should follow April or try to stop Jenny here. She clutched the dagger harder until her knuckles turned white, and the handle dug painfully into her palm. She'd never fought anyone, not for real — April had been the one to fight for Kimmie. Yes, she had a knife, but could she stab someone with it? Or would she freak out, like when Cheryl shoved her into a gym locker?

Freaking out is my signature move.

But Jenny had killed two people already with this same dagger, Maisie and Noah. And she'd let Sheila turn Kimmie's friends against each other, watching them die one by one while she pretended to be confused

If Kimmie failed to stop Jenny here, whether Jenny killed her or wounded her, April would be on her own, in the forest, in her bright red dress that would get easier and easier to see as dawn came.

It was safer to stay ahead of Jenny, to put herself between Jenny and April, either as a distraction or as a human shield.

Kimmie raced for the tree line. Prickly weeds scratched at her calves and ankles, and small stones sliced the soles of her feet. Behind her, Jenny swore, but Kimmie didn't dare look back to see how close the other girl was.

Almost there. The sky overhead was starting to pale, a warning that the sun was coming. Too late to save us.

But just in time to make it easier for Jenny to find them.

Kimmie pushed herself to run faster.

Moments later, she burst into the woods, stumbling over a gnarled root as she was enveloped in near darkness. April was somewhere ahead of her, running as fast as she could. Kimmie hoped she wouldn't stop, that she'd run forever.

A branch slapped her in the face, scratching her cheek. She stopped and blinked through the tears that welled up, wishing her eyes would hurry up and adjust. But at least the carpet of wet leaves and pine needles were cool against her throbbing feet.

As soon as she could see the outlines of trees around her, she started moving again.

Kimmie had to slow down as the trees grew closer together, but she forced herself to keep going, even though her lungs were burning and her legs felt like they were made of lead. She tried to stop panting, or at least to do it more quietly, but she was desperate for air.

She forced herself to stop and listen. She heard Jenny's heavy boots thudding on the wet ground and another curse followed by a squeaky sound. She slipped.

But then, behind her, she heard twigs snapping and leaves rustling. Jenny was catching up.

Kimmie hurried deeper into the forest, looking for some cover, a bush, or a tree that would hide her while she waited for Jenny to pass by. The closest she could find was a tree whose trunk might be thick enough to hide her. But could she make it before Jenny caught up to her?

She stumbled over a rotten log, then over another root. Her ankle turned, and pain shot through it. She moaned, then clamped her hand over her mouth.

But it was too late. She heard Jenny's boots stop. Kimmie froze, trying to slow her breathing, willing herself to blend into the forest.

"Kimmie?" Jenny called. "We're on the same side. You just can't see it."

Kimmie crouched down, then crawled slowly toward the tree, biting the inside of her cheek to keep from crying out from the pain in her ankle.

Made it. Kimmie scuttled around the tree, putting it between herself and Jenny's voice.

"Revenge won't be enough. She'll have to kill you to shut you up," Jenny added.

Kimmie huddled against the tree trunk and tried to make herself as small as possible. She brought the dagger up in front of her like she'd seen people do in movies, but she didn't feel any safer.

Jenny's boots crunched wetly on the leaves as she came closer.

"I know you're there," Jenny said. "I can hear you breathing."

Kimmie's heart was pounding so hard she was sure Jenny could hear it too.

She looked around frantically for a better hiding place

A spot of red caught her eye. A scrap of fabric from April's dress was caught on a branch of a small bramble bush a few feet away.

If Jenny saw it, she'd know she was on the right track. But if Kimmie moved, Jenny would see her.

She had to protect April first.

"Don't make me hurt you," Jenny said. "We can both have what we want if you'll just help me."

Kimmie leaned out from behind the tree trunk, reaching for the red cloth, but her fingertips only came within a few inches of it.

Jenny crunched closer. So close that Kimmie could see her now, but she was looking the other way.

If she turned around, she would see the red cloth. It was now or never.

Kimmie lunged for the scrap of fabric with her free hand, snagging it just before she landed face down in moldy leaves. Then she rolled over to face Jenny as the other girl spun around, keeping the fabric hidden in her fist as she awkwardly pushed herself up to her feet. She pointed the dagger at Jenny's face.

"Get out of here if you want to live," Kimmie said, trying to sound like she meant it.

Jenny laughed and took a step toward her, grabbing a branch and pushing it aside to avoid a mouthful of pine needles. "If you were going to hurt me, Kimmie, you would've done it by now."

Kimmie limped backward, one step, then another, as Jenny advanced.

"You might as well give me the knife before you hurt yourself with it."

"Stay back." Kimmie glanced over her shoulder to see what lay behind her. A ravine, with steep sides, she couldn't back down into it without falling, and a storm-swollen creek rushing through at the bottom.

She was trapped.

She turned back to Jenny just as Jenny lurched forward to grab her.

Kimmie backpedaled, barely avoiding her grasp. She gasped as she came down hard on her sore ankle, only a couple of feet away from the ravine's edge.

Jenny stopped and held her hands out, palms forward. "I'm serious about the coven. If you help me catch April, we can get Sheila out of her, and the two of you can be together."

"You've been lying to me all night." Kimmie kept the dagger's point leveled at Jenny's face. "Why would I believe anything you say now?"

"You have the gift. When are you going to use it?"

The voice buzzed softly in agreement, but Kimmie didn't care. "I'm not taking advice from a crazy person."

Jenny's eyes flashed, and she took another step forward. "You saw the same things I did tonight. If I'm crazy, then you're crazy too."

If Jenny got any closer, Kimmie would have to stab her. Or plunge into the ravine.

Unless—

"You are crazy." Kimmie limped another step backward as Jenny's face twisted into a rictus of rage.

Kimmie steadied and braced herself. She couldn't flinch, or it would all be over.

"You're a crazy murderer!" she yelled. "Who deserves to be locked up in a psych ward! Where you can't murder anyone else!"

Jenny let out a strangled cry and swung at Kimmie — but Kimmie was ready. She ducked under Jenny's arm, and as Jenny stumbled forward, she pushed.

Jenny screamed. Her arms flailed as she fought to regain her balance, but it was too late.

She fell over the edge, tumbling down into the shallow creek at the bottom. She hit the water, and her head disappeared under the surface for a moment before she began to thrash, churning the water around her.

If she let Jenny drown, did that count as killing her?

Or did letting Jenny suffer the consequences of her actions leave Kimmie's conscience clean?

Was she just as bad as Jenny?

She heard a choking sound. Jenny had surfaced, still thrashing as she retched up dirty water.

Kimmie let out a shuddering breath. She wasn't a murderer. Not yet.

She hurried into the darkness and prayed that she'd find April first.

THIRTY

Y ou have the gift. When are you going to use it?

Jenny's words echoed through her head again. The buzz had been silent for a while, but she'd also ignored it when it had tried talking to her earlier.

If she asked it, would it help her?

She stopped near a tree big enough to hide behind, in case Jenny was close and closed her eyes.

"Where is April?" she whispered.

Nothing.

Disappointed, she opened her eyes and turned toward the next big gap in the trees.

The buzzing started again, more of a mosquito whine than the swarm of bees she'd heard before. Still set her teeth on edge, but at least it was cooperating.

"Which way?" she asked.

The whine intensified slightly, but it didn't say anything she could make out.

She sighed and turned to look left. The whine softened and faded out.

Figures. Maybe she had a gift, but she couldn't depend on it.

She turned her head to the right, and the whine came back, crescendoing like the mosquito had kamikazed itself right into her ear and gotten stuck there.

She took a step to the right, and the whine almost vibrated, like it was screaming at her. Yes, go that way!

More craziness. But it wasn't like she had any better ideas.

So she went right.

◆

Kimmie froze at the edge of the small clearing, listening for the sound of someone else moving through the forest. But all she heard was the distant croaking of a frog and a faint rustling to her right — a squirrel, maybe? She hoped it wasn't something more dangerous, like a wolf. Or a bear. Or a mountain lion. Were there mountain lions this close to town?

How hilarious would that be? If she'd managed to escape a murderous ghost and the insane witch who wanted to be possessed by her, only to die a perfectly normal death.

She clapped her hands over her mouth to stifle a laugh.

She didn't know how much longer she could go on. She was cold, wet, exhausted, and completely lost. Even if she found April, she had no idea how much further the forest went on or where they'd come out. On the highway, halfway to Shady Vale? Or somewhere with people who might help.

She looked at the sky overhead, which had gone from black to midnight blue to something paler. Sunrise was almost here, which meant it would be harder to hide from Jenny. Kimmie did not doubt that she was still out there.

As she turned away from the clearing, her foot kicked and touched something soft that gave — unlike the firm flex of pine needles or the squishy sinking of wet leaves pressing into the mud.

Fabric. She looked down and saw April's dress, wadded up and half buried under the pile of leaves Kimmie had stepped on.

Was it luck, or had her gift brought her here?

Didn't matter right now. All that mattered was that she was closer to April.

April was fleeing through the forest in her bra and panties. But for once, Kimmie didn't blush at the thought. She imagined April peeling the dress off, alone and terrified and freezing her ass off, willing to give up what little warmth it gave her to be less visible. She must've seen that the sun was rising too and realized how easy it would be for Jenny to see her through the underbrush, even at a distance. It was almost as bright as the orange vests that hunters wore to keep from shooting themselves.

Oh shit, when did hunting season start?

Did they have to worry about getting shot too?

Getting shot would still be a hilariously normal death.

This time, the laugh was bitter. It sounded a lot like Jenny's laugh.

No. She was not going crazy. She was going to save April and tell the sheriff that Jenny had killed all her friends. Then she would return to her normal life, which she would never take for granted again.

"Which way now?" she asked the mosquito whine, which had faded to a high-pitched whisper once she had started moving again.

She began to turn in a slow circle. The mosquito whine got louder, then peaked and started to fade. Kimmie turned back in the other direction until the whine peaked again and started that way.

She made her way through the forest, following the sound of the mosquito whine. Every step hurt, and every step took more energy than the last. She pushed herself to go faster, ignoring the sharp twigs that scratched at her bare legs and the low-hanging branches that scraped at her arms and face.

When she felt she couldn't go any further, she heard something rustling ahead.

Hope surged inside her chest. She was so close to finding April — but would they be able to escape together?

Or was she about to walk into Jenny's ambush? She picked up her pace, ignoring the burning of sore muscles and stabbing pain from small cuts on her face and arms.

Whatever happened, she wasn't going down without a fight.

✦

Kimmie squeezed between two trees and emerged into a small clearing to see April in a black lacy bra and panties, her pale skin covered with bloody scratches and purple-black bruises much newer than the greenish one Kimmie had seen on her thigh earlier. Her damp, disheveled hair hung in dirty strings, with dead leaves and pine needles tangled in it.

April shivered as she reached for the branch of a tree, then froze as she caught sight of Kimmie.

For a moment, Kimmie thought she might run. Then she whimpered and held one hand out to Kimmie.

Kimmie ran to her, pulling her into a hug with one arm while keeping the dagger in her other pointed away from them both — she didn't dare set it down, even for a second, and risk Jenny sneaking up on them and grabbing it.

"I found you," Kimmie whispered as she hugged April tighter. "I found you."

April trembled against Kimmie, and her skin was so cold. Hypothermia? People died of that. But she had nothing to cover April with except her dress, which was too thin and wet to do much good. They couldn't afford to stay in one place to share body heat, either. They had to keep moving until they got someplace safe.

April started to pull away, and Kimmie let her go. But then April grabbed her hard and kissed her, forcing her tongue into Kimmie's mouth. This kiss was unlike their first — it was desperate, hungry, and full of frustration. Kimmie couldn't breathe under the smothering intensity of it. She pushed at April's shoulder with her empty hand, but April just kissed her harder, kneading the flesh of her back. No one had ever touched Kimmie like that before.

She wondered if this was how Spencer had kissed April.

But despite her discomfort, she felt a flush of warmth go through her. After being cold for so long, the heat was intoxicating. It made her head spin. Or maybe that was the lack of oxygen?

The buzzy voice rose in intensity with the warmth, taking on an anxious tone. Watch out.

Did that mean Jenny was sneaking up on them? Kimmie pushed against April again, harder this time. She gasped as April finally let her go, grinning cockily.

April was back. She looked at Kimmie like Spencer used to look at Kimmie. Like Spencer had looked at April at prom.

It felt wrong, but all of this was wrong. How could anything feel right until they were safe?

"Where's Jenny?" April asked. "Give me the knife."

Okay, maybe not quite like old April. But it was a relief to see her snap out of the childlike daze she'd been in since Jenny killed Zach. She was recovering.

But Kimmie wasn't ready to hand her the dagger after seeing her go crazy on Toby. The memory turned Kimmie's stomach. April's rage had been terrifying. She didn't ever want to know that side of her best friend again.

So Kimmie gripped the knife tighter and turned away as April reached for it, pretending she was listening for Jenny. "I pushed her into the creek, but she was alive when I left her."

"She's going to keep coming," April said.

"Not if she's in jail." A faint creaking behind her — was that a branch gently being pushed aside so it wouldn't rustle? "As soon as we get out of here, we're calling the sheriff."

"What if they don't believe us?"

"Jenny killed Maisie, but they couldn't prove it, so they sent her to a mental hospital. They're not going to believe her over us."

A squelching sound. It had come from the same direction as the creaking had.

She was coming.

"Get up in the tree," Kimmie hissed, taking a step forward and raising the knife.

"She won't go to jail. She'll kill us both." April shuddered, her eyes unfocusing and her mouth slack as she inched closer to Kimmie. "She'll kill us both."

If April lost it again, Jenny would have no problem taking her hostage — Kimmie was no match for her.

"Hurry up!" Kimmie pleaded. "You need to hide."

But instead, April took another step toward Kimmie, her arms out as if she planned to hug her.

Shit. How could she snap April out of it?

Before she could think of what to do, Jenny stepped into the clearing. She was spattered with mud from head to toe. The squelching sound had come from her waterlogged combat boots.

April whimpered and stepped behind Kimmie.

"Climb!" Kimmie said to April. Then to Jenny: "You can't have her."

She didn't look back, but the creak of a branch and the sound of April's fingernails digging into bark told her that April had obeyed.

"You think you're protecting her, but you're dooming her." Jenny took a step closer but stopped when Kimmie raised the knife. "As long as Sheila's controlling her body, April's trapped. A prisoner in her own body."

"Go away." Not persuasive or threatening, but what else was there to say? "Leave us alone."

"You're her best friend. You know her better than anyone. Is that—" she pointed, presumably at April in the tree behind Kimmie. "—the woman you're in love with?"

"You can't have her," Kimmie repeated.

She clenched her fist tighter around the dagger's handle, hoping that Jenny didn't notice the slight tremor. Her body felt heavy, but her head felt light like it might detach and float away. That was all she wanted was to float up into the sky and watch all this from above.

Safe. She wanted to feel safe. And she was afraid that she'd never feel safe again.

"Would the real April hide in a tree and leave you down here to die?" Jenny asked.

"Shut up."

But Jenny kept talking.

"Would the real April — the badass who killed her own brother to avenge her boyfriend, and let's be honest, that was badass." Jenny's smile said she genuinely admired April for that. "Would that April give up easily?"

Kimmie shook her head, but not because Jenny was right. Because this was a trick. It had to be. Jenny didn't know April. She wasn't going to turn Kimmie against April. "You don't know what you're talking about."

"Don't I?" Jenny glanced up and behind Kimmie again.

Kimmie resisted the urge to look too, which would mean turning her back on Jenny.

"Would the real April let you fight her battles for you?"

No. She never had before. But she'd also never killed anyone before.

"She's scared," Kimmie said. "She's not a wannabe witch like you. She's normal."

Jenny scoffed. "Because that's what normal teens do, spend prom night in the abandoned house of a murder victim. Wasn't that her idea?"

Kimmie wanted to defend April, but it had been her idea. "Shut up."

"That's how you know you're right when your best argument is shut up."

"Shut up!"

"Sheila can't afford to let anyone who knows her secret live. She'll kill you the first chance she gets."

Kimmie couldn't help imagining April shoving her down and bashing her head in with a Rubik's cube, spit spraying on Kimmie as fury transformed April's face into something demonic.

No. April would never do that.

Except she had, to Toby.

Who had deserved it.

But now Kimmie couldn't push the thought out of her head.

"I'm dead anyway," she said. "If Sheila possesses you, she'll use you to kill me. At least April would try to fight it."

"Once Sheila's inside me, I can control her. You'd be safe."

"Shut up!" Kimmie's hand trembled noticeably, and her head felt full of mud. There had to be a way to make Jenny disappear, but she couldn't think of it. "That's exactly what Sheila would say if she were possessing you."

"I can keep her from killing you," Jenny said.

"You're lying."

"I'm not." Jenny took a step closer and then another, forcing Kimmie to retreat until at her back was the trunk of the tree that April had climbed.

"I swear, I won't let her hurt you. Just put down the knife."

Jenny was close enough now that Kimmie could see the fervor on her face beneath the smeared makeup and the drying mud. Jenny wasn't lying. Jenny believed what she was saying.

But it didn't matter.

"No," Kimmie said. "You'll have to kill me."

"Don't make me," Jenny replied. "The rest of them had to die, but you don't."

She couldn't beat the other girl in a fair fight. And Jenny was beyond reason. What was left?

"All those scars from when you wanted to kill yourself," Kimmie said. "Why didn't you?"

Jenny's face collapsed into a rictus of grief. "I would kill myself right now if it would bring Maisie back."

Jenny dove for the knife in Kimmie's hand. Kimmie yanked it out of reach—

—but April dropped out of the tree, landing with a wet thud on Jenny. Both girls writhed in the mud as April tried to pin Jenny,

"No!" Kimmie cried as the buzzing swelled in her head, becoming deafening.

"Stab her, Kimmie!"

Jenny slammed her elbow upward, catching April's chin and throwing her off balance. April spat blood and wailed, clutching her face, as Jenny scrambled out from under her.

Jenny kicked at April's head, but her heavy boot connected with the arm April raised at the last second. Crack! April screamed and curled forward around her injured arm. Probably broken, Kimmie thought.

Jenny reached for April, and in a vivid flash, Kimmie could see how it would all end. Jenny dragging April away while Kimmie watched, frozen. April's body would be found in a ditch with her throat slashed.

And for the rest of her life, Kimmie would hide behind locked doors, terrified to leave her house, waiting for Jenny to come back and murder her too.

Kimmie screamed as she barreled forward, swinging the dagger as she put herself between Jenny and April. She felt the impact vibrate through her arm as metal connected with flesh, and sticky heat poured over her fingers as her momentum drove the blade upward, the painful jolt as Jenny collapsed, tearing skin from Kimmie's palm as the dagger's textured metal hilt jerked from her grasp.

Kimmie fell to her knees as Jenny hit the ground with a strangled grunt. She gasped and blood bubbled on her lips.

"You're dead," she rasped.

And then she went limp.

Kimmie screamed again, this time at the horror of what she'd done. She'd killed Jenny.

I'm a murderer.

She looked over at April, who crawled toward her, blood dribbling from her lips as she breathed in short pants.

We're both murderers.

"I didn't mean to," Kimmie repeated.

"Yes, you did," April said, crawling closer. "She was going to kill you, and you saved me."

Kimmie stiffened. Realization dawned as she jerked herself away from April.

Was she even really April any more?

"It's over," April murmured as the faint wail of a siren wafted through the trees. "You saved me. Everything's going to be okay now. It's over."

But Kimmie knew it would never be over.

THIRTY-ONE

"I'm trying to figure out how ten kids having a party turned into eight murders and a house explosion." Sheriff Williams was asking for the truth, but Kimmie was pretty sure he wouldn't be happy if she gave it to him.

She glanced at April, wrapped in a gray wool blanket and crying into a tissue from the box that the female deputy had retrieved from her car. She hoped April would get the details right. They'd only had about fifteen minutes to rehearse their story before the sheriff arrived responding to a neighbor's report of a gas leak explosion.

Beyond April and the deputy, paramedics brought body bags out of the house on a stretcher, one at a time. She saw them struggling to get the latest into the back of their van and numbly wondered if it was Noah or Spencer. Or maybe Jenny.

Did it even matter? They were all the same, just bodies in bags now. Tears welled up in her eyes.

She took a deep, shuddering breath. "At first, we thought someone else was in the house with us. By the time we realized it was Jenny ...."

She stared at the side of his car, watching blue and red flashes play across the Bellwether Sheriff's Department logo. She hadn't realized it would be this hard to get through the story without slipping up. All she wanted to do was scream and sob until someone comforted her the way she'd comforted April. But she had to make sure that no one blamed April — because when the sheriff talked to the other kids at school, he was going to find out that staying at the Bain house had been her idea.

"We walked in on Jenny as she was slitting Noah's throat ...."

She choked up for real this time. Noah had been nothing but a gentleman to her all evening. He'd done his best to protect them until the end, even though he could barely sit up because of his concussion.

"I can't believe he's dead!" she wailed, and her grief was genuine.

The sheriff patted her awkwardly on the shoulder until her wailing collapsed into sniffles. "Whenever you're ready, how did Jenny die?"

This was the easy part because it was true. As long as she kept it simple. "We ran out into the forest to escape, but she found us. When she tried to kill April, I grabbed her wrist. I was trying to take the knife away, but I accidentally stabbed her."

"You said before that you'd just met Jenny tonight." The sheriff was making notes on a small pad of paper. Did that mean she'd contradicted herself? She didn't think so, but it was getting harder and harder to think.

"Did she say anything to indicate why she wanted to kill you?"

"She said she'd spent time in a psych ward after her sister Maisie died. She showed us these scars ..." Kimmie ran her finger up and down her arm to show where Jenny's scars had been and shivered. "I think she did it to herself."

"She just told you that?"

"We were playing truth or dare," Kimmie lied.

The sheriff sighed and closed his notebook. "I was the one who found her in that house. Her sister's body, too. The younger one was catatonic, and we couldn't get anything out of her. We couldn't prove she'd killed Maisie, but we couldn't prove that she hadn't. Either way, it seemed like the best thing, her parents putting her in a mental hospital."

"How did she get out?" Kimmie asked.

"We're checking on that. Who invited her to the party?"

"She was Toby's date. I think he met her online." Kimmie sniffled, and felt another sob coming. She used it to sell another lie. "I just feel so bad for her."

Sheriff Williams sighed, and she couldn't tell if he was unsatisfied with her answers or just upset in general.

"You said that lightning caused the destruction to the corner of the house, but the storm stopped hours ago."

He glanced at April. Because he was eager to see if her version of the story matched Kimmie's? Or because he was hoping to wrap this up?

Then he asked, "Are you sure you didn't smell gas at any point in the evening?"

"Maybe," Kimmie said. "We were burning candles."

He nodded like that was the missing piece he'd been looking for.

"You get comfortable. Your parents are waiting to go with you to the hospital. You both need to get you both checked out." He turned to walk back to the squad car. Then, he couldn't help adding: "I know a haunted house sounds cool to you young folks, but abandoned properties are dangerous, even in a small town like this one. I hope you ladies have learned your lesson."

"Yes, sir. We'll never do anything like this again, I promise." Kimmie murmured. wanting this to be over.

A few moments later, Kimmie saw April walking towards her. She didn't say a word, just sat down beside her, grabbed Kimmie's hand, and squeezed it.

Everything is going to be okay, Kimmie thought, as long as I'm with April.

EPILOGUE

One month later …

◆

Kimmie dabbed the glue stick on the back of the butterfly she'd cut out from one of the nature magazines that Orderly Jeremy had left for them, then carefully placed the butterfly at the center of her collage. Cherubs fluttered in the corner. She had cut them from a wedding planner's ad and a crown from an article about the new Snow White remake. It was the evil queen's crown, but Kimmie had added a tiny opal from a picture of a ring to make it hers.

The most challenging image to find had been the sword — the closest she could come was a samurai's katana from another movie ad.

She smiled as she examined her work. A Queen of Swords collage for April. Her mother had promised to deliver it to the facility where April was staying.

Soon they would be together again. Kimmie had been marking off the days on her calendar with the Sharpie she'd "borrowed" from the nurse's station and hidden in her dresser. Only one more week and her three months were up.

Then she and April would be together for the rest of their lives.

She'd been good, taken all of her medicine. The cottony fog in her head was a relief after the screaming nightmares she'd had every night up until the trial. The fog made it harder to remember the blood. And the water, although Kimmie still felt the fear rise through her and squeeze her throat whenever she had to bathe.

She remembered her friends' names, but she couldn't remember their faces, making the haunted house seem far, far away.

Best of all, the medicine made the buzzy voice in her head finally stop talking to her. She never wanted to hear that voice, not ever again.

Kimmie couldn't remember why she hadn't wanted to come here. She'd argued with her mom while they waited for everyone else to realize that Jenny was the bad person and that April and Kimmie had never wanted to hurt her.

Jenny had made them hurt her.

All Kimmie could remember now was that she'd been afraid before but wasn't scared now. She was happy. Except for how much she missed April.

Once they let Kimmie out, she'd still have to see Dr. Springer weekly. And she'd probably keep taking her medicine. But at least she'd be able to see April again..

April's grandmother had been so mean to them both in the press. She said April and Kimmie had hurt Toby. Or at least, they hadn't helped him. She even said that April should go to prison forever. That had made Kimmie upset but she knew April was brave and had the guts to stand up to her grandmother now.

But Kimmie wasn't as brave as April. Kimmie had cried when the cops asked her questions. She cried at night because she missed her friends. And she cried in the morning because no matter what medicine she took, the dreams wouldn't leave her alone.

Kimmie had been so sad that her mom thought she should stay in the hospital for a while longer.

Mom had been right. The extra time helped. She hadn't had a single dream for the past two weeks.

Orderly Jeremy came over to the table and tapped her on the shoulder. "You have a visitor, Kimmie."

Mom typically came on Tuesdays, and Kimmie's calendar said today was Thursday. Was today special? Had she forgotten?

She followed Orderly Jeremy out to the visiting room.

April! She almost yelled, but then she remembered that Orderly Jeremy liked it when she used her inside voice.

Kimmie ran over to hug her friend, who was wearing outside clothes. April smiled wide.

"I missed you so much!" Kimmie said. "I'm making you a collage."

"I missed you too." April held her hand, and Kimmie blushed. "You're all I can think about."

April stared at her, as Spencer used to stare at April, making Kimmie blush harder. April was so beautiful, and she'd never looked at Kimmie that way before.

The way Kimmie had always wanted her to.

But there was something different about April, too. Not sad and scared, like Kimmie looked all the time. April seemed...older. And a little bit farther away.

Maybe that was how April looked: sad.

"Do you—" The question was hard to form, but she forced herself to focus. "Do you still miss the others?"

April smiled, and for some reason, she looked a little scary. "No, Kimmie, only you."

"Is your grandmother still mad? For Toby?"

It wasn't the best way to ask, but if Grandma Patricia was still mad, then April was still getting punished. And Kimmie worried about her. She had been so sad about everything before.

"Patricia fell down the stairs last week, right after I got home. She's in a coma."

No one had told Kimmie that April's grandmother was sick. Weird. "How?"

April leaned closer and whispered like she was telling Kimmie a secret. "It's just Warren and me now. He's learning his lesson."

Then April's smile was all teeth. "I said I'd get him back, and I did."

Now Kimmie knew why April's smile was so frightening.

It was Sheila's smile.

Sheila, the scary ghost.

"No no no," Kimmie chanted. "I killed you. I killed you. I killed you."

"You saved me," said April. "And I'm going to save you."

"I killed you!" Kimmie almost yelled, but just in time, she remembered that the ghost was a secret. Believing in ghosts would keep her here forever.

April bared her teeth at Kimmie again.

"Your friend's mind can't support my full powers, but yours does. Your skill and my gift? We're going to be invincible." April smiled and took Kimmie's hand.

She squeezed it hard enough to make Kimmie's eyes water.

"I'm going to make us immortal," she said. "We're going to be together forever."